FIVE ways to FINISH™

MICK MORRIS MYTH SOLVER

#2 BIGFOOT... BIG TROUBLE!

written by K.B. Brege

illustrated by D. Brege

ISBN 13: 978-0-9774119-1-7
ISBN 10: 0-9774119-1-5

The trademark Five Ways to Finish® is registered in the U.S. Patent and Trademark Office.
First Printing Paperback edition – July 2006

Special acknowledgements to Mick, Katie, and Karl.

www.KarenAndDarrin.com
www.MonsterMyths.com

Printed in the United States of America
10 9 8 7 6 5 4 3 2

With love to our son who inspires us to stay young at heart through laughter and play everyday. To all of our family, friends, and fellow artists who color our world with wonder…and to all of those who believe.

Table of Contents

#2 BIGFOOT... BIG TROUBLE!

Chapter One

The Lizenbog had me tied up! This time it would be the end of me, until I realized I was only dreaming.

I woke up to find that we were all safe in the Myth Mobile.

Whew! What a relief. I thought to myself as I looked over to see Sissy and Nathan both sound asleep in their bunks. I laughed when I looked to see the only thing tying me up was my blanket, it was wrapped around me like a sausage casing.

But then it got weirder, I could swear that I smelled sausage. I could! I rubbed my eyes and looked at my watch; it read 9:00 a.m. I climbed out of my bunk, took one look in the mirror, and decided the first thing I should do is take a shower.

After cleaning up I tiptoed outside, hoping not to wake Sissy and Nathan.

"Mick, there you are sweetheart. How are you feeling? You've been sleeping since seven yesterday evening." said Mom.

"I have?" I asked.

"Mmmhmm, you fell asleep right after dinner last night," answered Mom.

"I think that's a first." said Dad jokingly.

I never went to bed so early, and I *never* slept in past seven o'clock in the morning. I like to get up bright and early.

Dad was busy cooking eggs and sausage over an outdoor grill, it smelled great.

"Hey, we were getting worried about you guys. Where's Sissy?" asked Uncle Hayden as he walked up.

"I'm starving! Where is some food?" We heard Sissy's voice as the door to the Myth Mobile flew open.

"Guess that answers my question," joked Uncle Hayden.

I was keeping my fingers crossed Sissy would stay cool, and not turn into the spoiled brat she was before our alien myth-solving mission in Roswell. She had proved me wrong by being totally brave and helpful there.

"You guys must've had some fun out in the desert to be so tired," remarked Dad as the Myth Mobile door opened again. "Ahhh…and here comes the last of the musketeers."

We turned to see Nathan, and couldn't help but burst out laughing. His pitch black hair was standing straight up, and he had forgotten that he was only wearing his heart covered underwear.

2

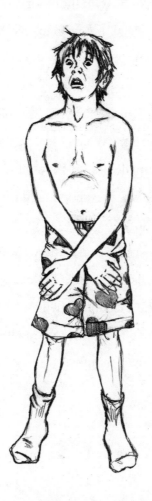

He came strolling out of the Myth Mobile, as we continued staring at him while laughing hysterically, he realized something was wrong. He stopped and slowly looked down, then screamed and bolted back into the Myth Mobile.

"Not funny!" Nathan hollered from inside, which made his absentmindedness even funnier. He was super-smart technically, but could be extremely forgetful in other ways. When Nathan came back out with his clothes on we couldn't help but tease him, as we all sat down for a delicious breakfast.

"Oh, have I got a surprise for you." said Dad.

"Cool, I love surprises! What is it?" I asked.

"Delicious, homemade orange marmalade," Dad said as he opened up the jar, stuck in a spoon, and lifted out a dripping, gooey orange blob.

I felt myself almost gag, and I knew I wasn't alone. Sissy turned her head in disgust, while Nathan covered his eyes. It reminded us of the Lizenbog aliens we had just narrowly escaped from, and the orange gooey drool that constantly poured out of their mouths.

"Oh … OK, no orange marmalade fans here," said Dad as he piled the gross, orange stuff on his biscuit.

After breakfast we cleaned up and secretly made jokes about the orange goo. It felt good to laugh about the last myth-solving mission. But what we didn't realize was what was ahead of us on this trip was going to be anything but funny.

Chapter Two

"Let's get this show on the road," said Dad. "According to this map northern California is about another thirteen hours from here."

"California?" squealed Sissy in delight. "I've always wanted to go to California!"

"California?" I asked. "I thought we were off to Oregon. I thought we were tracking Bigfoot."

"First of all, we are not tracking anything – we are shooting a documentary cable show, Mick," said Dad. "And your mother thought it was Oregon because there have been so many Bigfoot sightings there as well. It's actually right next to the Oregon border, Bluff Creek, California."

Dad had used my name at the end of a sentence, and that usually meant that he wasn't thrilled about something that I had just said, or did. He had been giving me the 'good old dad look' every time we talked about Roswell at breakfast. I couldn't even give a hint of an idea that we had actually met good and bad aliens. Because whether he believed me or not, it would be the last time we ran off to discover myths on our own.

"Awesome! Awesome! Awesome!" exclaimed Sissy.

"What is awesome?" I asked.

"We are going to Hollywood. I will get to meet movie stars." Sissy squealed.

There it was, the totally girl, everything in pink, ridiculous Sissy. "Yuk," I thought to myself. She had returned in full force.

"We are *not* going to meet movie stars and we are *not* going to Hollywood." I snapped.

"Yes we are. Your dad just said so," Sissy giggled.

"Yeah, we're going to California, but not Hollywood," I laughed. "Not all of California is Hollywood. Tell her, Nathan."

"Uhhh…I don't think I really want to get in the middle of this," said Nathan.

"Please, Nathan, tell her," I begged.

"Oh, OK…Sissy, I live in Los Angeles. LA, near Hollywood, but it is completely different from where we are going. It's overcrowded with nothing but freeways, cement, movie stars, and people who want to be movie stars. Northern California is nothing like that at all. You won't even feel like you are in the same state. It is all mountains and thick forests; it's beautiful and mysterious. It has some pretty wild places, too. And, where we're going it's nothing but small towns.

"Really?" Sissy asked, depressed for a brief second, but then quickly changed her mood as she stared at Nathan and smiled, "So, since your dad is a big-time director, tell me, tell me, tell me, just who have you met that is famous?"

"Well, I have met a ton of stars," Nathan replied, as they walked to the Myth Mobile talking.

"That's your cousin," Uncle Hayden said as he laughed and shook his head.

Yeah, my cousin alright, I thought to myself, and now she was going to hog my best friend all the way to Northern California talking about movie stars.

Mom and I finished loading the supplies back into one of the huge storage compartments located under the Myth Mobile.

"Not that one, honey," Mom said as I opened the wrong compartment, "this one."

"Oh, OK. But this one is completely empty, Mom. What do we keep in here?" I asked.

"Dad just likes to make sure that we have some extra space."

I knew sometimes my dad had a certain way of doing things that to me just didn't make sense. He always said someday I would understand. I didn't know how right he was going to be.

Chapter Three

We had been on the road for quite awhile. Luckily the movie star conversation had stopped, especially since it wasn't really one of Nathan's favorite subjects.

As the son of a famous writer, his mother, and his father – a big-time director, he had seen and heard enough about LA to last his whole life. He always said he just wanted to lead a normal life, even though myth-solving missions were anything but normal.

The scenery had already changed, and it was looking much thicker, greener, and scarier. We continued to follow the twisting turning roads through the mountains.

We had started to see a few signs that advertised Bigfoot souvenirs. It made me think about some of the crazy things I had read about Bigfoot. Like the fact that people recorded hundreds of sightings and encounters with the beast for the last 200 years. And not just in the United States, but also in Canada, Europe, and Asia. There were also tons of different names for it, such as Sasquatch, Yeti, and even Skunk Ape. Bigfoot was said to range in size from seven to twelve feet tall and weigh over 900 pounds. It was always described as an apelike human covered in coarse brownish-black hair from head to toe. There have been people who found its gigantic footprints and made plaster casts of them.

Some people say that they filmed the beast; there was even a famous film of a Bigfoot woman walking in the woods from years ago. But many people say it was just a hoax. People still argue as to whether it's real or not. Nobody has ever proved whether Bigfoot exists, well not yet anyway – that was our job.

The Uncover Cable Station had done a lot of stories, but this time we would be filming longer than usual. Nathan's dad, Mr. Juarez, and the film crew would be meeting us in Bluff Creek. They had to make a stop to drop off the Roswell footage in LA.

It had started raining, and now it was coming down harder and getting dark outside.

Whenever we film on location it's always on a pretty tight schedule. It usually takes something major to slow us down.

"I know we haven't discussed this," whispered Nathan, "but I can't keep it in any longer, I just can't believe what happened in Roswell."

"Shhhh!" scolded Sissy. "They'll think we've lost our minds."

"We'll never-ever-ever tell them," I answered.

"What's all the whispering I hear back there?" asked Mom as she walked to the back of the Myth Mobile. She had a curious look on her face, the one that says she is about to question us.

"What do you mean, Mom?" I asked as my mind raced... *I can't lie. I never lie. They taught me not to, and she can tell if I'm even stretching the truth a little bit. Nathan knows this about me,* so as I quickly bent over pretending that I was getting something out of my backpack, Nathan cut in.

"Oh, Mrs. Morris, we were just...uh...just talking about the...uh..."

Oh no! Now he was stuttering. My mind raced. *What can I say? What can I say?*

11

"Oh, for crying out loud." Sissy interrupted. "Would you two quit bumbling and spit it out?"

Our mouths dropped open; we were in shock as we turned around and stared at Sissy. I knew she couldn't be trusted. I knew she was back to her old tricks again. She was going to spill the beans and tell everything. They would think we were all crazy, either that or total liars. I would never be able to go on another myth-solving mission again in my life. It felt like everything was moving in slow motion as the words tumbled out of Sissy's mouth.

"We, and when I say we, I mean all three of us," Sissy stammered.

It felt like forever.

"Nathan, Mick, and I…well…uh, we were just whispering about how we, yeah we…uh, were going to plan my Dad's birthday party. That's it! It's in a couple days and yeah, it's going to be his birthday. That's it."

At the exact same time Nathan and I breathed a huge sigh of relief.

"So that's the big secret?" Mom asked. "It's a good one. I almost forgot myself. Well, why don't the three of you decide what type of surprise you would like to have and when we get to our next location we'll plan it together."

"Sounds great, Mom. Great idea, Sissy." I replied excitedly. Sissy had saved the day.

"OK," said Mom as she turned to walk to the front of the Myth Mobile. She believed Sissy. Then she suddenly stopped, turned around, and walked back toward us. We held our breath.

"Also, I want to make sure everybody stays buckled up and in their seats. This storm is getting worse. We are going to try to find a place to stop and wait out this rain for awhile. Dad heard the weather report and it's not clearing up anytime soon," Mom continued as she again turned and went back to the front of the Myth Mobile.

"Whew! That was close," I whispered. We all breathed a sigh of relief, and all went back to our reading and music.

Chapter Four

The storm was getting worse, way worse. It felt like the Myth Mobile was swaying back and forth. Lightning was crackling across the dark sky, making it look like eerie daylight outside for an instant.

Uncle Hayden was driving and said he couldn't see more than two feet down the road. The rain was coming down so hard and loud it sounded like gravel pelting the RV. Every once in awhile thunder boomed so loudly it would startle us and we would all jump.

"OK, it's getting really dangerous now, we have to find a place to stop," said Uncle Hayden sounding scared.

"It looks like there's a sign up there on the right, but I can barely see it," exclaimed Mom.

I wiped the fog from my window and tried to see. We were going very slowly now. It was one of the worst storms we had ever driven through.

"Uncle Buckey's Tavern Exit 13, five miles ahead— left on Reeker Road," read Mom.

As we passed by the sign I could see it was old, green, and faded. It was lit up by a single light bulb that flapped from a pole in the rain.

Exit 13 and a storm like this, it was getting really freaky. I knew it had to be really bad for Mom and Dad to stop at an out-of-the-way place like that.

The Myth Mobile slowly pulled off Interstate 5 and onto a deserted road. Uncle Hayden was doing his best to control the Myth Mobile while zigging and zagging on the muddy road to avoid giant potholes.

Thank goodness for seatbelts because the Myth Mobile was bouncing all over the place. Nathan looked concerned. But Sissy continued to listen to her music with her headphones on while reading her magazine. Every once in awhile she would loudly blurt out a part of a song, trying to sing but she sounded awful. I didn't know what was scarier, her singing or the storm. Now that we were off of the main road, it was darker than ever. The Myth Mobile continued down the twisting, turning road.

"This is creepy, where are we anyway?" hollered Sissy with her headphones on as she looked up.

Just then the Myth Mobile made a sudden turn as Uncle Hayden pulled into a parking lot, and stopped. We quickly unbuckled and went to the front. The headlights shined on an eerie old, dark, neglected log cabin with a rusted out sign that read, 'Uncle Buckey's Tavern.' There was an 'Open' sign hanging crookedly on the door. Uncle Hayden turned off the outside lights while we followed Mom

15

to the back of the Myth Mobile. She opened up one of the seat storage units and began passing out yellow raincoats with hoods. I thought it was pretty cool that we were always ready for anything, especially since it was raining even harder now.

We jumped out of the Myth Mobile trying to dodge puddles as we ran to the front door of the tavern. It was almost impossible to see where we were going because of the pounding rain, but we could sure smell something.

"Yuk! What's that awful smell?" yelled Sissy through the rain.

"Are you sure you want to stop here?" I asked.

"It'll be fine," hollered Dad as we all gathered together on the front porch of the old cabin.

The smell lingered in the air and I couldn't imagine ever eating here if it always smelled like this. It was like a combination of old garbage, gym socks, and skunk all mixed together.

The place looked abandoned except for the small glow of what appeared to be candles inside. The rusted metal Open sign clanked against the door when Dad gave it a pull. It opened. We stepped into a small hallway. It was covered in aged Pine paneling and rain soaked carpeting. On one side of the hallway was another beat-up sign.

"All welcome! Come on in! Dine with us and you'll never be thin." Mom read aloud. We laughed, but I couldn't tell if our laughter was because of the craziness of the sign or out of our nervousness in this spooky place.

It felt like it was something out of a horror movie. Like any minute some maniac was going to jump out at us. But before I could even think much about it, a man's face poked out of the dark and we screamed!

Chapter Five

He was a sinister looking old man, with shaggy, unkempt gray hair. His wrinkled, old face looked like he hadn't shaved in days; he was wearing a worn flannel shirt and overalls. When he spoke, his voice was gravelly and his right eye didn't move with his left eye. He leaned in toward us.

"What can I do ya folks for?" he asked suspiciously.

"Eh-hem," Dad cleared his throat, a sure sign he was nervous. "We've been traveling for awhile, and the roads have gotten extremely dangerous. We saw your sign and thought we would get a bite to eat while we wait for the storm to clear."

"Ohh, hmmm...Well it ain't gonna clear anytime soon!" the old man barked.

"Oh, I see," answered Dad, completely puzzled by the strangeness of the man. Mom immediately stepped up and I knew there was no way she was getting back into the Myth Mobile right now.

"Are you still serving dinner? If not, could we just get a cup of coffee or a soda?" Mom asked politely.

"Don't serve no soda." The old man barked in the most improper English.

Just as Mom was going to reply, the floor creaked from inside the restaurant and there was a figure of a woman in the shadows.

"I suppose I can get you all some grub," said the old man glancing toward the figure. "Wipe yer feet before yous come in. I'm Uncle Buckey, your host." His tone of voice had changed, but there was something very shady about him.

Sissy looked at me trying not to laugh as she mouthed the word *host*.

We pretended to wipe our feet on the soaking wet carpet and followed him into the dark restaurant. Then he stopped suddenly, and we all bumped into each other. He turned around staring at us like we were a bunch of idiots. Then with his one eye looking at us and his other eye going the other way Uncle Buckey asked, "That your big fancy bus out there?"

"Yes, Sir, it is," Dad answered proudly.

"Hhhmmph." he retorted while grumbling something under his breath as he continued walking.

"Find yerself a comfortable spot. I'll git Sophie." said Uncle Buckey.

Oddly enough, the creepy tavern had only about fifteen tables and a long, old saloon carved wood bar that stood against the back wall. It looked completely out of place, like it was from the Old West. There were some candles dimly lighting the room, and some old posters and mirrors with advertising on them that were hanging on the walls as decorations.

We sat down at a rickety table with a candle burning in an old cup. It was weird because we were the only people in the whole place. It was like they were open for business, but didn't want anybody coming in, or he didn't. Things were getting creepier by the minute.

Chapter Six

From the back of the restaurant, where the woman was standing in the shadows, we could hear muffled voices. Then another figure emerged from the darkness. It was an older woman with curly gray hair. She was wearing a flowered smock. As she approached our table she spoke so fast that she barely took a breath while slapping plastic menus down on the table.

"Welcome to Uncle Buckey's Tavern. Did he tell ya no 'lectricity? Well, if not I'll tell ya, no 'lectricity. So's no use lookin' at them there menus unless you have cat eyes and can read in the dark. Heeeee Heeeee!" Her weird laugh pierced the dark silence, "Cat eyes. Anyways, I got some fresh bread, just baked this mornin', and fresh lunchmeat from Farmer Nate down the road."

"Farmer Nate," I whispered, while Sissy and I made faces at each other and pointed at Nathan because of the name "Farmer Nate."

"That'll be fine," answered Mom, giving us a look while we tried hard to hold back our laughter.

"Ya all in town for the carnival or just passing through? Kids love..." Sophie continued.

21

"A carnival?" Sissy interrupted while jumping up and down in her seat.

"Awesome!" Nathan and I said at the same time.

"Jinx you owe me a soda," I said.

At that very second Uncle Buckey popped out of the dark again, right next to the old woman.

"No!" Uncle Buckey yelled so loudly that we shuddered. "No carnival here!"

"Why yes there is … Well, OK it starts tomorrow but …," Sophie answered back.

"No. No there ain't." Uncle Buckey said sternly.

"Maybe it's not like any carnivals that they's used to, but it's a carnival just the same, and lemme tell you this one's really interesting," Sophie continued.

"Really? Interesting? How so?" asked Mom, as she smiled warmly at Sophie. Mom could charm people with her smile, and the woman instantly moved closer to her.

"Well, it's kind of like those old sideshows, ya know, the ones that used to travel around in the 1800's with the freak shows. Freak shows, that's it." Sophie explained excitedly to Mom. "And this one claims to have a bearded lady who does tricks with her beard, imagine that. And, a sword swallower, and a lot more."

"Is that so, Sophie?" Mom asked cautiously.

"Yep, and that's not all," said Sophie, talking even faster as she leaned in over the candlelight, her eyes widening as she whispered, "They even claim to have a real Son of Bigfoot!" Immediately our laughter stopped.

"Awww, Sophie's just makin' that stuff up to tease ya. Ain't no carnival," Uncle Buckey said as he quickly stepped in, nudging Sophie to the side. He then lifted his knarled hand up to the side of his head and slowly made a circular motion, as if to say that Sophie was crazy. But as he did, his weird eyes went in two different directions and he was the one who looked crazy.

"Now just what is wrong with you, Buckey? You know there is! You're the one who put the poster on the wall." Sophie said, as she pushed him out of the way and pointed across the dark restaurant.

It was hard to see where she was pointing, but at the exact moment when we all turned to look thunder and lightening struck, lighting up the entire room. There on the wall were four white corners, remnants of where a poster had been torn away!

Frustrated, Sophie turned and looked at Uncle Buckey. Her lips tightened and she stormed away. Once again he made the crazy hand motion and then quickly followed her through the dark restaurant.

"Son of Bigfoot!" "Are you kidding?" "Could it be real?" We all started talking at once. Mom was saying it would make great opening footage, if there was really a carnival freak show.

Dad tried to calm everyone down. Finally we all quieted down at the same time except for Sissy, and she yelled at the top of her lungs to be heard, "Waaaayyy tooo spooky here!" Oops."

"OK, I know this whole thing seems pretty weird," agreed Dad. "It's probably because of the bad storm and the fact that we are all tired. Hopefully we can get back on the road after this and get away from this strange place."

What Dad didn't know was that the strangeness had just begun.

Chapter Seven

Sophie brought out the homemade sandwiches. They actually looked pretty good and ended up tasting great. But something was different about her; she seemed oddly quiet.

"Thank you for your patronage," she said awkwardly. "We will be closing soon. Is there anything else I can git you?"

"No, thank you," answered Dad while pulling out his wallet and handing Sophie money for the bill. Once again she disappeared into the darkness. We ate quickly. Then Uncle Hayden went out to the Myth Mobile to check the weather on the radio. He came back in soaking wet.

"Looks like we are going have to camp here for the night, the storm has worsened and there is a severe thunderstorm warning in effect until two o'clock this morning. I don't want to take a chance hitting any washed-out roads. We can get an early start in the morning since we're only a couple hours away from Bluff Creek," said Uncle Hayden.

"Don't allow no camping here," said Uncle Buckey as he once again popped out of the darkness. It seemed like he had been spying on us.

"I have had about enough, Buckey!" Sophie snapped angrily as she came from behind him. She began removing the plates and utensils from the table. Then unexpectedly she held up a knife in her hand as she looked at Uncle Buckey while we froze in our seats. "They ain't travellin' tonight!" She then calmly placed the knife with the dirty dishes, and it looked like Uncle Buckey's googley eyes were about to pop out of his head with fear. "You can stay parked in our lot. Just back away from the front of the building and ya need to leave before our breakfast rush," Sophie continued.

"No problem, thank you." said Dad, relieved.

"We'll be out of here bright and early," added Mom.

We put on our raincoats back on as we quickly left the restaurant and the freaky, old couple. We ran through the pouring rain and puddles to the Myth Mobile.

"Freak show footage would be awesome for the opening." insisted Mom, as we got inside and took off our drenched coats. "That is, if there really is an old freak show and carnival nearby."

Nathan, Sissy, and I went quietly to the back while listening to Mom, Dad, and Uncle Hayden talking.

"We'll find out the closest town in the morning," stated Dad.

"There's a nearby town, called Willow Creek, I saw it on the map," said Uncle Hayden, "That's probably where

26

the carnival is."

"I think it's called Creepsville, that's what I think," said Sissy, frightened as she jumped into her bunk and pulled the covers over her head.

"What d' ya think, Mick?" whispered Nathan, as our parents continued talking.

"Something's really weird about those two and this whole place. I don't know, but I think I believe her about the carnival and Son of Bigfoot." I said.

"Yeah, me too," agreed Nathan.

"I think we just might be on to something here." I replied.

"Ithhiithhhrrrbttthhccraaeee," Sissy mumbled from under the blankets.

"What?" I asked.

Sissy poked her head out from under the covers. "I think they're both crazy."

Suddenly the lights went out and it was pitch black. Sissy screamed and the lights came back on immediately. Mom, Dad, and Uncle Hayden began laughing from the front of the Myth Mobile.

"Hey, that was a really bad joke." insisted Nathan.

"OK, OK, we're just trying to get you to settle down now," Dad said.

"Not funny." I stated.

27

There was no way that I would be able to sleep now. I quietly reached for my backpack and got out my Mick Morris flashlight and my book entitled *Strange, Weird and Unexplained Myths*. As I began to read more about the myth of Bigfoot, the rain came down harder and I slowly fell asleep.

I woke up in the middle of the night to what I could swear was a strange howling sound. Then it sounded almost like moaning through the pounding rain. But nobody else woke up, so I pulled the covers over my head. I tried to ignore my wild imagination and the scary sounds as I fell back asleep.

Chapter Eight

It couldn't be morning already. It was still dark outside, but the rain had stopped and it sounded like an engine running outside of the Myth Mobile. Then it went silent, like it had stopped right behind us.

"Mick, do you hear that?" Nathan whispered groggily.

"Yeah, let's see what's going on," I replied sleepily as I slowly climbed out of the bunk, trying not to wake anyone else.

I couldn't believe that nobody but Nathan and I had heard it. We slowly tiptoed to the very back of the Myth Mobile to look out and see what the noise was. We carefully peeked out of the blinds. Right there on the road in front of Uncle Buckey's, stopped behind the Myth Mobile, was an odd looking old truck. It looked like it was the front part of a semi truck without the trailer, and there were two passengers in the front cab.

"Mick, what is it?" Nathan asked.

"I don't know," I whispered. "It looks like two guys in an old semi truck, but it's hard to see." I slowly and carefully slid the window open to see if we could hear what they were saying. The truck was about four feet from the Myth Mobile.

"...ver Show? That show could mean trouble for us." I heard a raspy man's voice say.

"Yeah, no kidding, I think that we better take care of things," said the other man's voice. I could feel Nathan tense up next to me. Then the truck slowly pulled away.

"What do you think is going on around here? Ver Show? Ver Show? I know they must've been reading 'Myth Solver Show' on the side of the Myth Mobile," Nathan whispered.

"Nathan, you're right! But we better keep it to ourselves and not even tell Sissy."

"Too late. And uh, excuse me, but if it weren't for me you two might still be dangling from a cylinder in Roswell right about now, or did you forget?" asked Sissy, who had snuck up behind us.

Sissy was right. We were a team, and we had better stick together if we were going to solve this mystery. I started to tell them what I knew about Bigfoot, that there had been sightings across the world for at least 200 years. That Bigfoot was also know as Yeti, Sasquatch, and many other names depending on where they had been spotted. And some of the accounts said they were dangerous beasts, and others said they were harmless and trying to hide.

"The beasts? Hundreds of years?" Sissy asked, surprised. "So then are you telling me there could be more than one of these giant creatures?"

"Well, logically, yes. If they've been spotted across the globe for hundreds of years, it's highly unlikely that there is only one," Nathan replied calmly as Sissy interrupted.

"OK, I get it. I get it, but what else do you know?" questioned Sissy.

"The footprints that have been found of Bigfoot throughout the centuries range in size from fourteen to nineteen inches long," I said, as Sissy stared at her foot.

We didn't realize how long we had all been seated in a circle on the floor talking about Bigfoot. We were totally absorbed in our conversation. Suddenly there was a huge shadow looming over us!

Chapter Nine

"Excuse me, guys I didn't mean to startle you. But just what time did you characters get up?" asked Dad.

"Oh, uh, a little while ago," I replied.

"Morning kids," said Mom as she walked into the kitchen. "Anyone want muffins?"

"MMmmmm, sounds good." said Sissy.

"Sure does," said Nathan.

"Count us in." I replied while looking at my watch. It was already 6:00 a.m. and I knew Mom and Dad wanted to get an early start. I knew they didn't want to occupy Uncle Buckey's parking lot with our huge Myth Mobile when his breakfast rush hit. By the time we ate, got dressed, packed, and ready to go it was 7:30 a.m. But the parking lot was still empty, except for us.

We waited inside the Myth Mobile with Uncle Hayden while Mom and Dad went in to thank Uncle Buckey and Sophie for letting us park there overnight. A few minutes later Mom and Dad were already walking back to the Myth Mobile.

"Well, we left them a note," said Mom sounding puzzled.

"Seems like they're gone, the place is all locked up," added Dad.

As we slowly pulled out of the parking lot, I looked back at the broken-down, scary restaurant, and I could've sworn I saw the curtains move.

"Look." said Nathan as he pointed toward the back of the tavern. Even though it had been dark, it looked like the same truck that had pulled up next to the Myth Mobile before dawn. Now we knew that something very strange was going on.

Uncle Hayden, Mom, and Dad had decided to try to find the carnival. We were heading toward the nearest town called Willow Creek. The scenery was lush and green with thick forests covered with vines. We were surrounded by huge mountains on all sides. We passed a sign that read

'Now Entering Humboldt County Bigfoot Country.' It sounded familiar. I grabbed my book and looked it up. Sure enough, it mentioned that Willow Creek, in Humboldt County, was considered the capital of Bigfoot sightings.

Seconds later we were pulling into Willow Creek and right in the middle of the town square was a gigantic wooden carving of a Bigfoot. Whoever carved it had made it look like they knew exactly what a Bigfoot would look like. It was a huge, hairy ape-like creature and it was at least fifteen feet tall.

Dad was now on the phone calling the road crew. He called them last night to make sure they could meet us if we took any detours on the way to Bluff Creek. They had stopped in LA to drop off the footage and got on the road last night. They, too, had to stop overnight because of the storm but now were not too far behind us. Dad gave them directions to meet us in Willow Creek.

Uncle Hayden found a parking spot, and there were already lots of people in town. As we passed by, they would just stop and stare and point at the Myth Mobile. I guess I would too; with the wild graphics of aliens, ghosts, and especially, the painting of Bigfoot on it.

Nathan, Sissy, and I went with Mom to the general store to see if we could find out more about the carnival,

34

while Dad and Uncle Hayden phoned the crew again with directions.

I felt like we had stepped back in time. The general store was super old. It was a long, narrow building with old wood shelves that lined the sides. The shelves were filled from floor to ceiling. It had everything, tools, fabric, food, toys, and even penny candy.

A woman in a checkered apron with a name tag on that read 'Judy' was behind the counter. She politely asked if she could help us, and Mom asked if there was a carnival nearby.

"Why yes there is," she answered. "Follow me, there are posters right …"

Just as we turned around to follow her Uncle Buckey was standing right behind us!

"Mornin' Buckey," the woman said, sounding annoyed. "I'll be right back …"

"Need my supplies right now, Judy." snapped Uncle Buckey as he stared at us. It was almost as if he had never seen us before.

"Oh, alright Buckey, well ma'am, there are posters just outside this building, and all over town. They have directions to the fairgrounds on them. That's where the carnival is," Judy said as she pointed outside.

Buckey sneered at us as we walked outside to find the posters, but once again everywhere we looked, there were only four white corners left. It was as if someone had come into town and ripped down all of the posters.

Chapter Ten

Now we knew that someone was hiding something, and we were going to find out what it was. We climbed back into the Myth Mobile and told Dad and Uncle Hayden what happened. Whoever was tearing down the posters didn't know that we had an awesome GPS satellite system right in the Myth Mobile. It could give us directions to wherever we wanted to go. Uncle Hayden typed in Humboldt County Fairgrounds. It came right up. We had the directions and Buckey couldn't stop us.

We buckled up and as we pulled away we could see Uncle Buckey walk outside the store. He stood and stared at us. Uncle Hayden purposely went in a different direction, around the block, just so Uncle Buckey wouldn't follow us.

As we hit the dirt roads, the traffic got heavier and we could tell we were getting closer. Then, around a bend, there it was.

"Oh, how fun! An old-fashioned country fair." squealed Sissy.

Once the Myth Mobile was parked I asked Mom and Dad if we could wander through the fair.

"As long as you take the walkie-talkies and promise to stay together. Don't get out of sight of the Myth Mobile," Mom said.

"I promise."

"We promise," said Nathan and Sissy while putting their Myth Solver backpacks on.

The three of us took off down the main stretch of the fair. It was wild! It felt like we had stepped back in time.

There were a few rides scattered around, like a Ferris wheel, a merry-go-round, and a few others. But it was nothing at all like the rides at amusement parks we were used to. Sissy stopped to get pink cotton candy. There were tons of games, such as toss the ring on the glass bottle, darts, and squirting games, and lots of the old-time creepy mannequins in glass boxes that would move and spit out cards. We stopped at the Fortune-Teller box and each one of us got the same fortune, 'Beware of strangers.'

"OK, that's the weirdest fortune I've ever got." stated Sissy as she stared at it.

"Yeah, I have to agree. It's pretty creepy they're all the same," exclaimed Nathan.

"Here, I'm going to try again," I said. Just as I was about to put a token in the slot I was startled when an odd-looking man, with a thick black moustache, a red-and-white striped vest and a derby hat on came up to me.

38

"Step right up!" he bellowed in my face. "Right over here, young man." He began pulling me by my shirt.

"Hey! Let go of me!" I yelled.

"Yeah! Let go of him," Sissy hollered.

"What are you, afraid? Yes, you are, afraid that I'll be able to guess your age or your weight, little man? Don't be shy, I'm never wrong. And if I am, then you yourself can go home with one of these lovely prizes…That's right, boy. For a token you can win!" he shouted right in my face.

"No thanks." I said as I tried to walk away while straightening my shirt. I was totally embarrassed as people gathered around, and Sissy and Nathan had started to laugh.

"Do it." said Sissy. "You could win one of those pink stuffed unicorns for me, please, Mick. Puh-leeeez."

"Give it a try, Mick." encouraged Nathan.

"No. You do it, Nathan," I said.

"Awwww…what are you, shy? Yep folks, we got a shy one on our hands," the odd carnival man now yelled louder than ever.

"Oh, alright, already." I said as I dug a token out of my pocket.

"What's it going to be, shy boy? Your weight or your age?" he asked.

"My age," I snapped. I was mad now; I was no shy boy. I knew that I was tall for my age and I could probably fool him anyway.

"Your age, your age, hmmm," he said as he closed his eyes and made a weird face like he was concentrating. "You are twelve years old, that's it … twelve years old."

"Sorry, Mister I'm ten," I said as I went to grab a stuffed animal for Sissy.

"No, you're not!" he snapped at me angrily.

"Yes, I am." I smiled.

"Yes, he is!" said Sissy. "Now give us our prize."

He slowly moved away so I could get a pink stuffed unicorn for Sissy. He was mumbling something under his breath and staring at us as we ran away laughing.

We passed by all the other games, food, and rides and then came upon a row of dozens of tents. In front of every single tent there was a big sign that had an old cartoon painting of some sort of carnival freak. The nightmare had begun!

Chapter Eleven

It was tent after tent of total weirdness. It was just like the old traveling freak show that Sophie from Uncle Buckey's Tavern had told us about.

"Boy, that carnie kind of freaked me out," I said.

"Yeah, there was something really bizarre about him," agreed Nathan.

"What's a carnie?" asked Sissy.

"A carnie is short for a guy who works at a carnival."

As we started to walk past the 'Tattooed Man from Head-to-Toe' tent, another carnie with weird shaved hair started to yell at us to come inside.

"Want to go in, guys?" asked Sissy.

"Nahhhh … we can just see him at the local mall," I said, laughing.

"Yeah, I guess you're right," agreed Sissy.

"Look, Mick. 'The 10-Foot-Tall Man' tent. I wonder if he's on a basketball team yet?" laughed Nathan.

"If not, I'm sure he will be soon and I hope that it's our team." I replied.

"Look." said Sissy, "the 'Fire-Eating Man' tent. C'mon, let's go see if he really eats fire."

41

"Why not?" I replied. As we walked up to the tent, a weird-looking woman dressed in black leather with lots of piercings took our money. She didn't say a word; she just motioned with her head for us to go in. There was something sinister about every person that we came across.

Inside there was a small round stage with a table. On the table was a bottle filled with yellow liquid and a couple of torches that looked like giant cattails from a swamp. There were some chairs, and we sat down in the middle row. Some other people filed in behind us. Then music started and an extremely pale, thin, bald man came onstage. He bowed as he took off a satin cape, which revealed that he was wearing only satin boxer shorts, matching satin ties around his skinny arms, and socks. Nathan, Sissy, and I tried hard not to laugh as we looked at each other.

The odd man picked up a torch and showed it to the crowd. He then opened the bottle and dipped the torch into it. Next, he took out a box of matches from his satin shorts pocket and held them up. After removing a wooden match from the box, he lit it by striking it against the side of the box. He then held the match to the torch.

WWWHHHOOOOSSSH!!! The torch immediately ignited. He did a quick little dance and then bent his head and body as far back as he could. He slowly put the entire torch in his mouth. He closed his mouth around it and then pulled it out. The flame was completely gone and the torch was smoking! We all applauded, but it was totally odd.

"Do you think he burns himself?" asked Sissy as we left the tent.

"I would say so, not something anyone with any brains should ever try," I answered.

Next was the 'Four-Legged Man' tent. We paid and went in. It was so phony. A man came out and danced around with what were clearly two fake legs with shoes and pants sewed onto his clothes.

"We were just ripped off," I said.

"No kidding," Sissy agreed.

After that was the 'Bearded Lady' tent.

"What do you think?" I asked.

"Why not?" answered Nathan.

We paid our tokens and went into another dimly lit tent. Onstage was a big lady in an old, tight blue-satin dress with her back to us. She had a tiny monkey that sat on her shoulder picking at her long brown, matted hair. The monkey started to act like it was throwing something at us; then the music started.

The big woman slowly turned around and sure enough, she had a five-foot-long beard. She started to play with her beard right in front of the crowd. She parted her beard down the middle and then tied a knot in the bottom.

The monkey climbed down her hair as she bent over; he then sat in the bottom of the beard as she helped him swing back and forth. Sissy, Nathan, and I just stared; it was the most bizarre thing that we had ever seen.

"Do you think that the beard was real?" asked Sissy as we left the tent feeling somewhat disgusted.

"I don't know," answered Nathan; it sure did look like she had a stretched-out chin."

"If it wasn't, and it was just glued on, it must've been some strong glue." I answered.

Either way, it was kind of gross and strange, like everything at this carnival.

Chapter Twelve

We walked past the 'Sword Swallower' the 'Two-Headed Cow' and the 'Siamese Twins' tents. The thought of some of them was creeping us out.

"Oh, we have to go into this one," said Sissy as she pointed to a sign that read 'Madame Varooshka can see your fate... Step right in before it's too late.'

"Another fortune-teller?" I asked.

"Yeah, c'mon this one's real." insisted Sissy.

"Why not? There aren't very many more tents," said Nathan.

As we started to go in a man that looked like a gypsy stopped us.

"One at a time for Madame Varooshka! say Igor," he snapped.

"We can't all go in together?" I asked.

"One at a time for Madame Varooshka say Igor!" he repeated himself.

"OK, I'll go first," said Sissy excitedly.

I was a little worried, letting her go by herself. But this tent was small; there could only be enough room for two people and a couple of chairs, and we would wait for her right outside.

Within three minutes, Sissy came out of the tent looking upset.

Next Nathan went in, while Sissy and I stood silently next to the big gypsy man who continued to stare at us. Again, within minutes, Nathan was out.

"Your turn, Mick," said Nathan seriously.

I slowly walked into the tent and was surprised by what I found. The entire tent was draped in sheer, dark fabric; it was lit by a few candles on a small table where the fortune-teller sat. There was a bookshelf next to her and on it was a teapot, some books, and a skull. The skull looked real, but I was sure that it had to be a fake.

As I approached the table, she quickly lifted her head. She was wearing a dark turban that was draped with jewels and gold. Her face had deep creases, her mouth was covered with heavy red lipstick, and her eyes were outlined in heavy black make-up.

"Seeet down, Meeester Mick Morrrris," she said as she rolled her *R*s in a thick, deep accent.

"Oh, OK, sure," I said, stunned that she knew my name. As I sat down in the chair across from her. On the table there was also a deck of cards and a crystal ball. It was like a scene out of the movies.

"Cut zee deck!" she snapped, and I jumped.

I slowly lifted the top half of the cards and placed
them on the table. She stretched out her thin, boney,
mummy-like arms and grasped the cards with her long,
blood-red fingernails. She quickly flipped over the cards and
placed them in rows.

"Oh no, zees ees not goud!" she said in her thick
accent.

"What's not?" I asked. My hand was still on the table
and she quickly grabbed it. I felt her long nails pushing into
my skin.

"You and your family must leave zeees place now!" yelled Madame Varooshka.

"Huh?" I said, confused.

"I see nazzing but grave trouble!" she continued while flipping cards over faster and faster. "Oh no, go now— goooo! Leave here and forget about myths or you will face horrors zat you have never known!" yelled Madame Varooshka as she stood up and pointed to the entrance of the tent. "GO!"

I quickly jumped out of my chair knocking it over, picked it back up. As I glanced up at her, her dark eyes were staring at me as she continued to point to the door. I tried to find the tent flap but couldn't my hands were shaking. She walked toward me, opened the flap, and I ran out. Right straight into Igor!

Chapter Thirteen

I bounced off of him and fell to the ground. He looked at me, shrugged, and then angrily walked into the tent.

"Mick, you alright?" asked Nathan as he and Sissy came running over.

"Yeah, I think so. Man was she creepy." I said.

"No kidding," said Sissy. "What did she say to you?"

We chatted about the frightening Madame Varooshka and realized she did almost the same thing to each one of us, except I was the only one that she yelled at. We were scared that she knew our names, and who we were.

We continued walking past a few more of the freak-show tents. Before we knew it, we had come to the very last tent.

"Just like Sophie told us." said Sissy, pointing toward the tent.

There it was! A huge white tent with a sign on it that read 'Step right up. See it right here. The one, the only, Son of Bigfoot!" It was the biggest tent of all and there was no one in front of it.

"Let's go in." said Sissy.

"We better get our parents first," I answered.

"Why? Did that Fortune-Teller spook you? You don't actually believe what she said, or in Son of Bigfoot, after seeing all of these phonies do you?" asked Sissy, laughing.

"Oh my gosh! I can't believe we are having this conversation again," I snapped angrily. "You remember, it's the same conversation we had before Roswell. You didn't believe in aliens either."

"Aliens are different!" Sissy barked.

"OK, you two. Who cares? It looks like it's not even open anyway, but let's go see," said Nathan. He was very good at being diplomatic; it probably had something to do with not being related to Sissy.

As we got closer to the tent the awful smell came up again.

"Whew! Do you guys smell that?" I asked.

"Pee-yoo." said Sissy.

"Just like last night at the tavern," added Nathan.

"Yeah, you're right," I said.

As we moved closer, the smell got worse, way worse. We had to hold our noses so we wouldn't gag. .

Chapter Fourteen

Just then a very sinister, greasy-looking man with bleached-blonde and black spiky hair, wearing dirty black jeans and white cowboy boots with a tight, white leather jacket that had weird, silver metal decorations on it, walked right toward us.

"Help you, kiddies?" he asked. As he spoke, the greasy guy picked his teeth with a toothpick. You could see that some were missing, and the teeth that he did have were brown. He moved nervously and something seemed oddly familiar about this guy.

"Uh…yeah, we wanted to see Son of Bigfoot," I answered, trying to act fearless.

"No kiddies allowed in to see Bigfoot, not without their parents," sneered the greasy guy as he spit brown stuff on the ground right in front of us, just missing our feet. My stomach turned at the sight of him, and the strange smell, which was now stronger than ever. I looked at Nathan and Sissy and they looked at me; we slowly backed away, then turned, and ran back toward the Myth Mobile.

Once we were in sight of the Myth Mobile we slowed down.

"Whew, that guy is really …" Nathan started to say, but at that second we saw the film crew truck pull up.

"Dad!" Nathan yelled as he ran toward the truck. His dad jumped out and hugged him.

"¡Hola hijo! ¿Como es usted?" his father said.

"¡Muy bien, papa! ¿Y tu?" Nathan replied, as they asked each other how they were in Spanish.

Nathan was thrilled to have his dad there, and it was great to see the crew. It now felt safer having our gang with us.

"Mickers!" shouted Dennis Hinkleson as he came out of the truck. Dennis was nicknamed 'Boom' because he operated the boom microphone equipment. He was one of the greatest guys that you could meet. Plus, he knew everything about myths.

"Dennis! You are on this shoot too?" I asked.

"You bet I am, little buddy! Just in case we run across any Bigfoot." Dennis said as he was interrupted.

"You might be mistaken for him!" laughed JB. JB stood for James Brunk who was the cameraman. We always thought that he was the coolest of cool and could do the funniest Eddie Murphy imitation; in fact, he laughed just like him. He loved to joke around. He also loved to sing and was constantly humming or tapping a tune. When he wasn't on location somewhere, he played drums in a jazz band.

"JB!" I laughed, happy and surprised to see him. His band had been cutting a CD so he hadn't been on location with us in quite awhile.

"Mick Morris, my friend. Slide me some," he yelled as he came over to greet us.

"Sissy, this is JB, the best drummer in the whole world." I said.

"Pleased to meet you," said Sissy as she curtseyed. Why she did weirdo stuff like that, I'll never know. But then JB bowed back the exact same way causing massive laughter.

"Oh my, likewise," replied JB. "So just what have you children been up to? When your mother called, she said that this has been a strange trip so far. Is she right? Or is it just that crazy Morris imagination of hers?"

"No, she's right," I replied.

"Yeah, no kidding," added Nathan. "There are some really creepy people around here."

"People? People don't scare us, just creepy aliens and monsters! EEEEeeeeEEEEeeee!" yelled Boom as he held his hands high in the air while wiggling his fingers like some giant monster.

Even though it was very funny, I shuddered at the thought of the frightening people we had come across. Nathan was right, they were creepy, some of the creepiest I had ever seen.

Chapter Fifteen

"Oh yeah, we have to take our parents to the 'Son of Bigfoot' tent," I said as Nathan, Sissy, and I ran over to where Mom was chatting with some of the crew.

"Hey Mom…Mom!" I said loudly, trying to get her attention.

"Mick, what is it?" Mom asked, stopping her conversation with the script supervisor, and angry that I had interrupted her.

"The greasy carnival guy, who I am now calling Greasy Guy, said that we could see Son of Bigfoot." I said excitedly.

"Great, honey, great. Have fun." Mom said as she began talking to the script supervisor again.

"No, you don't understand. You have to come with us."

"Wait a minute … did you say Bigfoot? Seriously? This could be the footage we need. Wait right here, I'll get your dad and the rest of the crew." insisted Mom as she ran back over to the trucks.

JB began grabbing one of his cameras out of a case while the rest of the crew started getting their gear. Mom,

Dad, Uncle Hayden, and Mr. Juarez began to follow Nathan, Sissy, and me. The crew caught up to us as we led the way past the amusement park rides, food, games, and the endless row of freak-show tents to the very last one, Son of Bigfoot. Oddly enough, the strange smell was gone and so was Greasy Guy.

As the crew buzzed about, getting ready to set up, there was an excitement in the air. They were thrilled to have something besides an old ranch and desert to film. Mom and Dad got in front of the camera; they were ready to roll.

"You know this here tent is private property and you can't be putting it in your fancy show," said Greasy Guy as he came strolling out of the tent.

"I thought that anything on community property was public domain," said Dad as he stepped up to Greasy Guy.

"Don't know anything 'bout no domain, but if you want to tape anything to do with my Bigfoot here, there's a fee," said Greasy Guy while picking his teeth and staring right in Dad's face.

"OK. How much?" asked Dad, unafraid.

"Two hundred bucks," replied the Greasy Guy as he spat on the ground again and began to look nervous.

Dad pulled out his wallet and peeled off two crisp one-hundred dollar bills and handed them to him. It was as if

Greasy Guy was just itching to take the money. He quickly snatched it out of Dad's hand.

Dad knew that the man couldn't charge him for filming on public property, but he didn't want to argue with him. Plus, he knew that Bigfoot, real or fake, would be some awesome footage for the show. The man stepped back and waved us past with his arm; as he did, his small leather jacket sleeve pulled up to reveal a skull tattoo.

We began walking to the entrance of the tent. This was it.

"Aaaaaaaooooooouuuuhhhhaaaaaaa..." A horrible, moaning sound came out of nowhere. We all froze.

Chapter Sixteen

But the sound wasn't coming from inside the tent. It sounded like it was farther away…like it was from deep in the forest somewhere. It was the same kind of sound that I could swear I heard in the middle of the night.

"What was that?" asked JB.

"I don't know. I've never heard anything like it." said Mr. Juarez.

"It's probably just carnival sound effects," said Dad.

We all walked into the dark, spine-chilling tent. Once inside it was hard to see because it was so dark. There were some old, beat-up, red velvet curtains and a crummy stage made out of plywood.

While the crew quickly lit the tent with portable lights, JB got the camera ready to roll and Boom hoisted the microphone over the stage while the audio man, Brett, did a quick sound check.

"Rolling," said Brett.

"Speed," said JB.

"Action!" said Mr. Juarez, and just as they were ready to film, speakers crackled and something that sounded like an ancient recording started to play and a light flickered on. *Step right up! Step right up! Welcome to Caswell's Carnival of Fiendish Freaks! Feast your eyes on the one, the only, living legend...You may ask yourself, is it man, or is it beast? That is for you to decide! From the darkest, deepest corners of the world we bring you – Son of Bigfoot!*

Sissy, Nathan, and I moved up closer to our parents as the old curtains slowly opened. There it was, the most ridiculous looking, fake, hairy costumed person that I have ever seen in my life. Everyone tried hard not to burst out laughing as the camera continued to roll. I knew we didn't expect a real Bigfoot, but certainly something a little more authentic than this.

Whoever was in the silly, old ape costume started pounding his chest and pacing back and forth on the stage while hooked to a giant metal chain, which was about the only thing that was real.

"Cut!" laughed Mr. Juarez, "well we've got some footage for fun, or we could possibly mix it into the opening with the village statue."

"That'll work," laughed Mom as Bigfoot stared at us while howling and pounding its fake chest.

As we left the tent, the man in the fake costume continued grunting at us.

"How ridiculous." said Sissy.

"Yeah, but something's not right," I answered.

"I'll say! That guy was anything but Son of Bigfoot," answered Nathan.

"That's exactly it." I said.

"What's it?" asked Sissy.

"They're hiding something," I answered excitedly. "Look, 'Son of Bigfoot' is what they advertise on the outside of their tent, right? But inside its some guy dressed up like Bigfoot."

"Yeah, so what?" Sissy questioned.

"So what? So nothing. Even the weirdo recording said Son of Bigfoot."

"OH NO!" Sissy immediately yelled.

"What? What's wrong?" I asked.

"I lost my pink unicorn!" cried Sissy. "We have to find it."

"Mick, I think that you're onto something here. They must be hiding something…heck, even if they're not, I'm up for a little pre-myth-solving mission. C'mon Sissy, we'll look for your unicorn later." Said Nathan.

While our parents and the crew were setting up to film more exterior shots, we asked if we could go see more of the carnival. We were determined to find out what was really going on; not knowing what horrible secret awaited us.

Chapter Seventeen

We hadn't seen Greasy Guy since Dad paid him the
two hundred dollars. Once we were out of site from our
parents, we ducked behind the tents and started heading back
to the rear of the Bigfoot tent. Sure enough, parked right
behind it was the cab of the semi truck, the same one that
had pulled up next to the Myth Mobile at Uncle Buckey's
Tavern.

We ducked behind another one of the tents and just in
time. From the back of the Bigfoot tent came the guy in the
Bigfoot costume. He was taking off his fake-looking
costume head. And right along with him was Greasy Guy.

"Yeah, just as we thought," I whispered.

"OK, so it's a phony Bigfoot. Did you expect
anything different?" insisted Sissy.

"Not sure—let's get closer and see if we can find
anything out."

We carefully ran down the side of the tent and then
quietly crawled under the heavy tarp into the Bigfoot tent.
We were on the inside wall of the tent from where they were,
and we could hear everything that they were saying.

"There it is!" whispered Sissy.

"Shhhhhh!" I said, while listening carefully. I didn't notice Sissy tiptoeing to the other side of the stage.

"What was that?" I heard Greasy Guy ask, and they were silent for a moment.

We froze, afraid they had heard us. I turned to see Sissy at the other side of the tent going after her pink unicorn that she had left on a seat.

"Not as long as those Myth Solver folks are around here…" I heard Greasy Guy continue.

"So how long do you expect me to wear this monkey suit?" asked a raspy voice.

Now we knew for sure they were the same men that were parked in the semi truck outside of the Myth Mobile in the middle of the night. I recognized the other guy's raspy voice. We had a feeling there was something familiar about Greasy Guy, but now we were certain.

"You better get back in there, in case they come snooping around again," said Greasy Guy.

"Oh alright, but what about the beast?" the other guy asked.

The beast! The beast?!? We couldn't believe what we had heard. Nathan and I looked at each other with our eyes wide-open, but we had to remain silent.

"I'll head back and check on him, then I'll come back to keep an eye on those Myth Solver folks RV. When they leave, I'll be back," said Greasy Guy.

"He's coming back into the tent; we gotta get out of here!" Nathan whispered fearfully as the truck engine started up.

"Sissy?" I whispered as I turned to see her walking towards us. "Sissy! Get over here fast!"

"What do we do now, Mick?" Nathan asked just as Sissy joined us.

"Quick! Under the stage!" I said.

"Whaaaa….?" Sissy started to say until I pushed her toward the stage and she began to crawl under it. It was just cheap old plywood and it was a tight squeeze. Luckily there were some old horse blankets spread out that we could lie on until the coast was clear.

"What are we doing?" whispered Sissy.

But I had no time to reply…we could hear the man directly above our heads.

Chapter Eighteen

Suddenly there were more muffled voices. It was Dad, Uncle Hayden, Mom, and the crew. *Whew!* They had come back into the tent to ask the phony Bigfoot if they could get a few more shots of him. Perfect! It gave us the chance to escape.

We quietly shimmied our way back out from under the smelly blankets and stage and ducked outside of the tent. We stayed as close to the tent as we could. We could see the dust from where the semi truck had been driven into the woods. It was down a path right next to the big, beat-up old trailer, the half of the truck that they must've used for transporting all the rides and games. The trailer had the carnival's name on it, 'Caswell's.' Now we had to find out what they were hiding.

"OK, that guy is going to keep an eye on the Myth Mobile, right?" I asked.

"Right," said Nathan.

"I guess so," answered Sissy.

"So we are going to have to split up and use our walkie-talkies, because we can't risk following that semi truck into the woods on foot and that guy seeing us. So here's my plan ..."

Once we had finished covering all possible situations, we ran back to the Myth Mobile. Just as we had hoped, Greasy Guy had made it back before us and was parked near the Myth Mobile. We made sure he saw us, while not letting him know that we saw him. We began talking loudly and laughed as we went inside.

Once inside, Sissy peered out of the curtains. "Looks like the coast is clear, he's got a newspaper."

"He can read?" Nathan asked.

"OK, we're out of here. Keep your walkie-talkie on," I said as Nathan and I went to the front and cautiously climbed out of the driver's seat side. Then we ducked down while making our way to the other side and slipped into the crowd of people.

"Mick? Nathan? Over." said Sissy.

"We're here, Sissy. Over." I replied.

"So far, so good. Got him covered. Over," said Sissy confidently.

"What's he doing? Over," Nathan asked.

"Looks like he's about to fall asleep. He keeps bobbing his head. Over," replied Sissy.

"Awesome. Keep in touch. Over and out." I said.

Once we got past the main area, we dropped out of the crowds and again snuck to the back of the tents. We headed toward the woods, past the steel gray trailer and down the path the truck took. We were determined to find out what "Beast" they were talking about.

"Ouuuuu, it's that gross, foul smell again," moaned Nathan.

"Yuk! You're right. What is that?" I asked, not knowing that we would soon find out. As we got deeper into the dark, scary woods, the truck path turned off into thicker, heavier brush. We continued to follow the trail as it wound up and around through the hills and trees.

"Look Nathan, it stops here." I said.

"Now what?" Nathan asked.

"We follow the smell." I replied.

The disgusting odor was stronger than ever.

"Look!" I pointed, but was hard to see, it looked like a giant square shape, sitting in the middle of a small clearing. As we got closer we could see that it was a box covered with a beige tarp and camouflaged with leaves, sticks, and branches. Nathan and I continued to climb through the brush toward the enormous box. Once we got close to it, we could see that it was a cage. We began to pull the leaves and branches off. I grabbed one side of the tarp and Nathan pulled the other side. It was big and heavy.

"How about on the count of three we both pull?" I asked.

"OK," answered Nathan.

"One, two, three!" we said in unison and pulled. The heavy tarp slid off. I gasped as we fell backward and Nathan covered his own mouth so he wouldn't let out a scream. There it was, one of the freakiest, hairiest beasts that I have ever seen in my life! The creature looked like it was part ape, and part human, with lion like features. It was completely tied up, its mouth covered with duct tape. It laid there staring at us with anger-filled eyes.

This is where the story stops. Now it's your turn. You get to decide which way you would like the story to go. That's right—there are *Five Ways to Finish* this story, and it's up to you to decide.

1) For a normal ending, go to page……..............68.

2) For a very scary ending, go to page……….111.

3) For a wild western ending, go to page…….147.

4) For a fun talk-show ending, go to page........171.

5) For a cool comic book ending, go to page....178.

Chapter One—Normal

"Oh my gosh!" I gasped in horror.

"Wha … wha … wha?" stuttered Nathan.

"I think…" the minute I tried to speak and the beast sat up.

It startled us so much that we both fell backward, again. The beast had now risen to its feet, and although it couldn't stand upright in the cage, it began moving back and forth, staring at us. It was the size of a big football player…but something told me that this beast was not fully grown.

"Nathan," I whispered as it watched our every move. "It looks smaller than I expected a Bigfoot to look, so this has to be …"

"Son of Bigfoot." we said in unison.

Immediately the creature began nodding its head up and down and fell to its knees.

"Mick, what should we do?" Nathan asked.

"I'm not sure yet, but I think it understands what we're saying."

"What makes you think that? That nod could have been for anything."

"Yeah, but his eyes…look at his eyes. It understands. Watch," I replied. Then I got up very slowly and cautiously moved closer to the cage.

"Can you talk?" I asked the beast.

He slowly nodded his head yes.

"Do you want to be free?" I asked.

Almost instantly tears filled his eyes while he tried desperately to get the tape off its mouth, but his hands were tied together. I moved closer to the cage.

"Mick what are you doing?!" Nathan yelled so loudly it startled me, and the beast began rolling around inside the cage.

"OK, OK, settle down. I am going to try to get that tape off your mouth," I gently told him.

"MICK! You could get hurt." Yelled Nathan, as the creature began to violently shake its head NO. "See! He's communicating with us. He's not going to hurt us. He knows that we're here to help him," I answered, and the beast began to nod its head yes.

Now we knew this giant, yet small, Son of Bigfoot could understand everything we were saying. I motioned for him to come to me. He immediately did.

"OK, this is going to hurt," I said. The duct tape was right on his mouth and hair. "On the count of three, I'm going to pull."

"Careful, Mick." said Nathan.

"Help me, Nathan." As Nathan got up, the creature was distracted for a second and put its head right next to the bars. I quickly put my hand into the cage near its massive face, grabbed a corner of the tape. Then, without even counting, I yanked the tape off as fast as I could. There was a horrible tearing sound. But even worse, the creature was now twisting and squirming in pain as it began rolling around the bottom of the cage.

"EEEEEyyyyaaaahhhhh!" he bellowed. It was the same exact sound I had heard before. Only this time it was so loud I swear that they could hear it as far away as New York.

"Shhhhhhh…Shhhh…" I tried to calm Son of Bigfoot down. He suddenly grabbed my arm, gripping it as tightly as he could. I could feel my circulation stopping as I tried to pull away. I was trying to get loose, but the beast was not going to let go!

Chapter Two—Normal

"Nathan, heeeellllpp meeee!" I screamed as its grasp grew tighter and tighter.

Nathan ran over as the creature moved closer to me. The smell was unbearable. Then, just as I thought it was going to bite my arm off, it looked me straight in the eyes and made some grunting sounds.

"Hold on a second. Mick, don't pull. I think that he's trying to communicate with you," said Nathan. I stopped struggling long enough to look in the beast's eyes, face-to-face. Nathan was right. He loosened its grip on my arm and nodded toward its hands. He wanted them untied. It slowly let go of me.

"Mick, don't tell me you are going to set it free?" asked Nathan, shocked that I would even think of such a thing.

"It'll be fine Nathan. He's harmless." I replied as calmly as I could. It's this or leave him here with those awful carnies. And to tell you the truth, I think I trust him more than them. Who knows what they'll do to him," I said, as the creature started nodding his head up and down. He understood what I had said to Nathan.

"Come here," I said softly, and the beast moved closer.

"Back up," I said, and he slowly moved away.

"See Nathan, we'll be fine." The instant I said it, the creature nodded its head yes again. "That's it Nathan, we are going to set this poor Bigfoot free."

"Give me your hands,uhhh…paws… mmm…whatever," I insisted. He moved his giant-sized hands toward me and I slowly untied the rope.

But now we had another problem. The bars of the cage were made of solid steel, and the wooden sides were secured with metal strips and giant bolts, and on the massive clip was a huge padlock.

"I think I have an idea," I said while digging into my Mick Morris backpack. I pulled out one of my mother's hairpins, always the best thing for picking a lock. That was until I looked at the lock. I realized that it was a huge ancient, metal one and it needed a skeleton key.

"OK, so much for modern locks," Nathan said. Suddenly the creature started pounding his chest and going crazy.

"Shhhhh," I insisted. "Someone will hear us."

"Look Mick, he's trying to tell us something." said Nathan excitedly.

Sure enough, the giant beast was jumping up and down and pointing to a nearby tree. It would run over to the lock on the cage, point to it, then run back and point at the tree. We walked over to the tree, and the closer we got the more excited the beast became.

"He knows there's something here to get him out of that cage," said Nathan.

"But, what?" I asked. "He could probably uproot this tree and pound himself out with it, but we can't."

At that exact moment, the creature started to shake his head no and point to the tree and then the lock. Nathan moved closer to the tree.

"I got it!" Nathan yelled. He climbed up the tree to the first massive branch and pulled down a rusted old skeleton key that had been hidden.

Nathan ran over to the cage without even thinking of the consequences, and he quickly unlocked the ancient padlock, then took it off. As we began pulling on the big, heavy cage door, the giant beast gave it a single push

74

and "BAM!" He knocked us both to the ground under the heavy plank door, trapping us underneath. We had made one big mistake.

Chapter Three—Normal

"I can't breathe, I can't..." gasped Nathan. He was stuck completely under the heavy wood-plank door. I was trapped under it too, but my head was poking out even though my arms were trapped under.

"Hang on, Nathan, just hang on." I gasped as I struggled in the sand to get out. Instantly the giant beast turned to look at me while still standing on top of us.

"Get off!" I screamed at him angrily but he looked at me, puzzled. Then he did something I couldn't believe...he jumped off of the heavy door and without any struggle at all picked up the door, making it look like a piece of paper, and tore it right in half.

I quickly rolled over to Nathan who looked unconscious. "Nathan! Nathan! Are you OK? Nathan! Wake up!" I cried while shaking him and slapping his face. I was scared out of my mind. What if something happened to my best friend?

"Whaaa...what? Where am I?" Nathan asked, as he slowly shook his head and opened his eyes.

"Nathan, are you OK? You scared me to death." I exclaimed.

"Wow, I must've started to pass out." Nathan coughed as he slowly sat up trying to catch his breath. "Uh-oh, where's Son of Bigfoot?"

I looked around and the creature was gone. He must've run away. Except for one giveaway that told us he was still nearby, the smell.

"He's somewhere around here…*sniff, sniff.,*"

Nathan nodded his head as I helped him up. We heard some rustling behind the enormous tree. We looked to see the beast peeking around the trunk.

"He's afraid," I whispered. "He must think he hurt us. It's OK, c'mon out. It's alright," I spoke softly as we began to move toward the tree while motioning for him to come out.

He sheepishly moved out from behind the tree with his head down.

"Look, there is no time to feel bad, OK? So you don't realize your own strength, it's cool, but right now we have got to get you out of here. OK? C'mon, let's go." I said as Nathan and I began to leave.

"Uh, Mick, I hate to tell you this but he isn't following us."

I turned to see the massive beast still standing behind the tree. We walked back to the tree.

"Look, me Mick, this Nathan," I said, while talking like Tarzan as I beat my chest.

Then the beast did something totally unexpected—he pounded his chest while saying what sounded like "Looookkkmmeeemmiicccc!"

Nathan and I burst out laughing.

"No!" I said, "Me Mick."

"NNNNAAAOOOO-mmmeeemiiiicccc!" Son of Bigfoot's voice boomed.

"Me Mick!" I said.

"MEEEMIIICC!" Son of Bigfoot repeated.

"OK, we are going to be here all day. Let me try," insisted Nathan. "Naaattthhhaaan, Mmmiiccckk," Nathan said while patting each of us on the head; then he pointed to the beast.

The beast let out what sounded like laughter and then patted its own head while saying what sounded like, "DAANNUUBBEEE."

"Danube?" I asked him.

"Danubeee," the Bigfoot responded.

"OK, can we just call you Danny?" I said as I pointed to him. He nodded his head crazily up and down.

"Great, Danny, that's great," said Nathan, "We have a Bigfoot with us named Danny." We laughed, and knew it was unbelievable that we were communicating with an actual Bigfoot.

"Mick, come in, Mick! Over," I heard Sissy say. Oh my gosh, I had almost forgotten about Sissy.

"Mayday! Mayday! Carnies on the move! Over!" yelled Sissy.

The sound of the walkie-talkie must've alarmed Danny because he began to jump up and down like crazy. He was pounding his chest and yelling at the top of his lungs. He had gone crazy and we were terrified!

Chapter Four—Normal

"RRRRgggghhhhhaaaahhhhh!" cried Danny.

"Sissy, Hi, Over," I said loudly into the walkie-talkie while trying to cover my ears.

"RRRJJJJJJAAAAAAHHHHHGGGGG!" Danny screamed louder.

"Oh my gosh, what's all that noise? Over," Sissy asked, frightened.

"It's Danny. Over," I replied.

"Who the heck, or should I say, what the heck is a Danny? Over," asked Sissy.

"No time for explanations now. Just tell me what's going on? Over."

"One of the other carnies came and said something to the Greasy Guy and he took off in the truck. I'm worried, Mick. Where are you guys? You better get back here. I think they know something and the other guy is now watching the Myth Mobile. Over." Sissy spoke so fast it was hard to understand her.

And the whole time Danny was jumping up and down screaming while covering his ears as Nathan tried to calm him down.

"OK. We're on our way back right now. I'll be in touch when we get closer. Over." I said.

"Hurry, Mick! I'm worried. Over," cried Sissy.

"Danny! Danny! Stop it." I insisted, trying to calm him down. He finally stopped yelling and jumping.

"OK, that's better. Now we are going to help you but we have to hurry. Let's go." I said as the three of us took off running out of the woods. But it wasn't long before we could hear a loud truck engine coming our way. We could see the look on Danny's face wasn't fear but anger.

"There has to be another path out of here." said Nathan.

The creature shook his head yes, and started heading another way. We followed him as closely as we could. Things were starting to get really scary. The brush was overgrown and taller than we were, as we tried to stay right next to Danny to get through it. We were going in the exact same direction as the other path, only hidden by the thick trees and vines. Danny had to crouch down because he was still visible. Moments later the truck passed right by us, going the opposite way. We had to move quicker. *It would only be a matter of time and those creeps would be onto us!*

Nathan and I were starting to lag behind, getting tired from climbing through the massive plants and vines. And it was hard to see in the dark shadows of the forest.

Danny noticed and he suddenly bent over and picked Nathan up and put him on one shoulder and then boosted me up onto the other. It was totally wild that this mythical creature understood us. But he wasn't really a myth anymore. We had met a real, live Son of Bigfoot.

"This is good. We aren't too far," I said as I could see the tents through the forest ahead.

"That's great, but now what do we do?" asked Nathan as we neared the edge of the forest. Danny stopped and helped us down. We had to make a plan. I hadn't really thought about what we would do with him, but he couldn't be seen out in the open. We looked at Danny as he picked up a stick and drew in the sand. What he was drawing amazed and shocked us.

Chapter Five—Normal

"It's a house." I exclaimed.

"And it looks like it has a river behind it…" said Nathan.

Danny nodded and pointed to the house, and then he made the river smaller.

"OK, not a river, smaller than a river," I said as Danny nodded his huge head again.

"A stream?" I asked, and Danny shook his head no.

"A creek?" guessed Nathan, and now we were onto something.

"Your house is on a creek." I said. "A specific creek?" Danny continued to nod yes. "Willow Creek?" He angrily shook his head NO.

"OK, it's on a creek. No, it can't be that easy, can it? Bluff Creek? Bluff Creek!" I yelled excitedly.

Danny stood up and started jumping up and down happily. It felt like the entire ground shook. But our excitement stopped when we could hear the roar of the truck approaching. Now we were really in trouble. Those dangerous carnies had to know by now that he had escaped.

They would know we helped him and they would be hunting us down.

The wind was blowing and the trees were rustling. Just what we didn't need was another big storm.

"Mick, come in. Mick. Over."

I heard Sissy. I thought for sure Danny would freak out at the sound of the walkie-talkie again, but this time he stood there calmly looking at it.

"Sissy. Over," I replied.

"Your Mom, our Dads, and the entire crew are back and they're packing up. They want to get going before another storm sets in, and they want to know where you are," Sissy exclaimed nervously. "I told them you we were playing hide-and-seek, ridiculous right? I know, but your mother told me to get a hold of you. Over."

That was it. That was all I needed to hear—the words hide-and-seek. I had an idea. We could hide him.

"We're coming in, Sissy, but I need you to help us. You know the storage bin under the Myth Mobile, the last one in the back? My dad keeps it empty but he locks it. The key is in the second drawer next to the fridge in the kitchen. Get the key and unlock it. Over," I said as we began moving out toward the edge of the forest. Danny followed cautiously behind us.

"Nathan I have an idea, but we have to move and fast. Time is precious…" as I explained my plan.

"Now what?" asked Sissy. "And don't forget there is still one of those carnies out there watching. Over."

"That's OK, now blow up an empty trash bag and act like you are putting trash in the compartment; then leave it unlocked, but closed, and watch for us from the front of the Myth Mobile. We will be coming through the parking lot. Whatever you do, don't let Mom and Dad see what you're doing. Over." I said.

"OK then, thanks for the easy task. No problem. Over," replied Sissy.

"Girls." I thought to myself and then quickly told Danny and Nathan the plan. It wasn't going to be easy, but if it worked we would be home free, or that's what I hoped.

Chapter Six—Normal

We ran as fast as we could to the back of the tents. One by one, we ducked and ran until we were finally behind the 'Son of Bigfoot' tent. Luckily nobody was around. We went inside the tent, and talk about luck.

"There it is, Nathan." I said as Nathan quickly ran over and began to put the Bigfoot costume on. It was way too big for him, but at this point it didn't matter.

"That'll work," I said as Danny grunted angrily at the costume. Time was running out. We hurried out under the back of the tent and kept creeping and hiding behind the tents. When we got to the last tent, we could see from a distance that the crew was packing up and Sissy was standing in front of the Myth Mobile. The other guy was watching her and the semi truck cab was now circling around with the Greasy Guy driving it. He was looking crazier than ever. This plan had to work. I was afraid for all of us if it didn't. Because it seemed like everyone at this carnival, and in this town was in on the Son of Bigfoot capture.

"Sissy, come in, Sissy. Over." I could see that she had heard us as she went back inside the Myth Mobile to talk.

"OK, this better be a good plan, Mick, because these wacko guys are watching our every move and waiting for you. Over." reported Sissy.

We crept behind the parked cars on the way to the Myth Mobile. We were almost there now!

"It will work. It has to. OK, we are coming in. Take your place Sissy. Over." I said

Perfect! Greasy Guy had pulled up and parked directly in front of the Myth Mobile and the other carnie went over to talk to him. Timing couldn't have been better. I gave Nathan the thumbs up as he cautiously moved to the end of the car that we were hiding behind. I could see Sissy taking her place toward the front of the Myth Mobile.

"In five, four, three, two, one, NOW!" I said as Nathan, now dressed up as Bigfoot, stood up, threw his hands up in the air, and ran toward Sissy.

We watched carefully as the carnie saw Nathan, grunting and hollering, running toward Sissy. Sissy began running in circles, screaming at the top of her lungs with her hands flailing in the air. Mom, Dad, Mr. Juarez, and the entire crew were running toward Sissy. Greasy Guy and the other carnie were running toward Nathan. It was total confusion. I couldn't watch anymore; this was our only chance. I gave Danny a tug and we were off and running, ducking around to the very front of the Myth Mobile, then around to the back on the other side. I could still hear Sissy screaming.

I pushed on the compartment. No way! It was locked. Did Sissy make a mistake and unlock the wrong one? I tried the other two next to them, they were locked too! And there was no key anywhere.

"Wait! Wait! It's me, Nathan! It's meeeeee... Fooled you. Ha, Ha, Ha!" I could hear Nathan yelling at the top of his lungs on the other side of the Myth Mobile. *But I was running out of time.*

I kicked the compartment one last time. It opened! It must've been stuck. I helped Danny get in. He looked scared but I assured him everything would be alright, yet in my heart I wasn't so sure.

Chapter Seven—Normal

I quickly ran around to the front of the Myth Mobile where everyone was yelling and arguing.

"Nobody stole your phony Bigfoot, Son of Bigfoot, or anything else, Mister!" Mom yelled angrily at Greasy Guy. "Look! Your silly costume is right here. It was just a childish prank."

"I am tellin' you, they took my creatuuurrre!" screamed the Greasy Guy.

"Nobody took anything. ¡Nathan rápido! Get out of that silly costume and give it back to the man," yelled Mr. Juarez.

Mr. Juarez must've really been upset because he was speaking Spanish, telling Nathan to hurry up. I managed to sneak into the group while Nathan was taking off the costume. I gave him and Sissy our secret nod.

"Hey, if there is a real Son of Bigfoot, how come all we saw was a guy in this silly costume?" asked Dad as the Greasy Guy immediately realized what he had been saying and backed away mumbling.

"Come on. Let's get going before the next big storm. It's time we left this weird place," said Uncle Hayden while leaning toward the carnies. The entire crew backed us up, staring angrily at them. Then Greasy Guy grabbed the costume out of Nathan's hands and left in a huff.

Nathan, Sissy, and I knew we better do something to lighten the situation and fast. We started laughing as hard as we could, and even though our laughter sounded totally fake, before long everyone was laughing along with us.

"You scared me to death, you monster." said Sissy, doing her best acting.

"Sorry, just having some kid-like fun." laughed Nathan, which was way too funny, because we knew that Nathan hated it when people called us kids. He always made a point of telling people that a *kid* is another term for a goat.

Either way, we were lucky that we pulled it off and had not gotten into trouble. We piled into the Myth Mobile as the crew got into the trucks. We slowly pulled away from the bizarre carnival.

Sissy, Nathan, and I were extremely happy to be leaving Willow Creek, but what was in store for us at Bluff Creek would make this place seem like a ride on the merry-go-round.

Chapter Eight—Normal

We had settled into the back of the RV, but there was one thing I didn't think of and that was the awful smell.

"Pee-yoo! What is that disgusting odor?" yelled Sissy with her headphones on.

Then I heard Mom say. "We forgot to empty the garbage bins in Willow Creek."

Nathan and I stared at each other.

"That's OK, we can do it when we get to Bluff Creek," Dad said. Nathan and I breathed a sigh of relief not even realizing that Sissy had been watching us.

"OK. I can't wait any longer to hear the rest of this story," Sissy whispered while taking her headphones off.

I held up my finger to my mouth to tell her to be quiet and motioned for her to move closer. Nathan and I told her about the cage and finding Danny, and what smelled so awful was Son of Bigfoot, and we were taking him back to where he was captured.

"No way!" Sissy blurted out.

"SSssshhhh, Mom and Dad will hear us," I said. "I know this all sounds unbelievable, but ...."

"Well, how do you know that he won't eat us?" Sissy asked.

"He won't eat us, he's a teenager," I replied.

"Oh, OK. Good, now I'm sooooo relieved. A teenager, oh that's good. Are you kidding me? I've seen boy teenagers eat an entire refrigerator of food." Sissy snapped sarcastically.

"He won't eat us, Sissy. We are just going to get him back to his family," added Nathan.

"Well, how do you know those weird people weren't his family?" asked Sissy.

"Very funny." I answered.

"He told us," said Nathan.

"He can talk? Then if he can talk, maybe you can tell him to take a bath," said Sissy snottily.

"OK, OK, fairly funny," I said.

But Sissy was right; the whole thing was unbelievable. We began to get our backpacks together, just to make sure we had enough supplies. We put fresh batteries in our walkie-talkies while planning how we were going to get Danny out of the Myth Mobile once we got there. We would hike with him as far as we could to get him back safely to his home. What we didn't know was that things were going to be a lot different than we planned. Our easy hike was going to turn out to be a horrible nightmare.

Chapter Nine—Normal

We pulled into a campground at Bluff Creek. By now the smell was making us sick to our stomachs. Sissy had stuffed tissues up her nose and looked ridiculous. We knew that we would have to move quickly before Mom went to empty what she thought was stinky garbage. I couldn't even begin to think about what would happen if Mom opened that compartment. As we came to a stop, we hurriedly put our backpacks on. We were ready to head out the door.

"Where are you guys off to in such a hurry?" Mom asked as she walked to the back of the Myth Mobile.

"Uh, well, umm…we thought we would do a little exploring while you interviewed those Bigfoot-sighting guys." I answered.

"OK, but check with your dad first," Mom said. "I'm not sure we will be here as long as we had planned, since we already shot a lot of extra footage today."

"OK, Mom." I said watching as she went into the kitchen to look for the key to the outside compartments. I quickly went to the front of the Myth Mobile to keep Dad and Uncle Hayden occupied.

Our plan was working. Sissy stayed in the back distracting Mom while Nathan ducked out the side door to go around and let Danny out.

"Hey there, Mickster," Uncle Hayden greeted me, "Ready to find a real Bigfoot and not just your buddy Nathan in a gorilla costume?" Then he burst out laughing, and so did my Dad. I did my best phony laugh, only I laughed a little bit too hard and a little too long, because when I finally stopped they were staring at me.

"Oh, uh, that was funny…uhh, eh-hem. Wasn't it?" I asked.

"Uh yeah," Dad answered, looking at me suspiciously.

"So Dad, Mom said to ask you if we could go exploring for a bit. Is that OK with you?" I asked hurriedly.

"Fine with me, but don't be gone as long as you were in Roswell. We were getting really worried. What do you think, Hayden, alright with you?" Dad asked while getting ready to get out of the Myth Mobile.

"OK by me, if you just keep an eye on your lively cousin," answered Uncle Hayden.

"No problem," I said as I walked to the back and gave Sissy a nod.

"Bye Mom," I said, giving her a quick kiss on the cheek.

"Boy, stingy with those lately. Please be careful and don't go into the woods. And, keep those walkie-talkies on. You never know, there could be a real Bigfoot out there somewhere." said Mom half-joking.

She didn't know how right she was.

Chapter Ten—Normal

Nathan managed to squeeze Danny out of the Myth Mobile compartment seconds before the crew pulled up. Nathan then ran toward the truck to talk to his dad, while Sissy and I waved at Mr. Juarez and the crew to distract them as Danny disappeared into the woods.

Nathan caught up to us just before we crossed out of the campsite as we walked along the edge of the forest.

"Danny?" I whispered into the woods.

"I don't know about this, Mick. This is one thick forest," Sissy whined.

"Dannnnnyy?" said Nathan. "I told him to wait for us."

"Oh, that's OK, I'm sure he knows his way around here," insisted Sissy.

"Let's not forget that we promised we would help him get back. We won't go too far; besides, we have a tour guide. We just might get to see more…," I was saying when I suddenly caught a glimpse of Danny directly above us in a tree as I pointed., "There he is."

Sissy and Nathan looked up to see Danny waving.

"Oh my gosh! He does *not* look like a teenager to me. He's the size of a full-grown man." Sissy said, frightened. "What does he really need us for?"

"He doesn't," I said. "But we might be able to get pictures of a whole Bigfoot family."

"Was that a little surprise that you had planned for me?" Sissy asked irritated, while Danny climbed down.

"Danny, this is my cousin Sissy," I said as Sissy cowered behind Nathan and me.

Danny grunted and began walking ahead of us deeper into the woods.

"Hhhhmmmpppphhh … his manners go along with his smell," snapped Sissy.

Danny turned and gave her a huge smile, revealing the biggest row of square, brown teeth I had ever seen in my life.

We continued walking as the woods grew thicker. Danny kept trying to touch Sissy's hair, and she kept slapping his hand away. He thought it was so funny, he kept doing it just to bug her. When she would yell at him to stop, he would mimic her whining sound. We were so busy laughing at the amusing situation we didn't even realize we were being followed. Now the fun and joking was going to end.

Chapter Eleven—Normal

"Did you hear that?" asked Nathan.

"No, what?" I asked.

"It sounded like twigs snapping behind us." He answered.

"Probably just..." I froze when I heard it. So did Danny. He looked around suspiciously. None of us saw anything, so we kept moving.

"Enormous, humongous footprints!" squealed Sissy, pointing to the ground right before we came upon a huge Redwood that had fallen and become a hollow, long tunnel.

"Those are huge." I said. "And check out that tree."

It looked like it had been carved out, but that was impossible. It crossed a beautiful, secluded valley next to a waterfall that tumbled far below. Danny motioned for us to follow him through it. We weren't sure, but he said it was safe. Once we were deep inside, almost halfway through, it felt like the giant tree tunnel was moving. I thought that it was just my imagination – but it wasn't!

"Hey, what's going on here?" asked Sissy nervously.

"Yeah, it feels like we're beginning to move," said Nathan.

"We are!" I yelled as I turned and looked at Danny who seemed to be as frightened and confused as we were. He came back to us and wrapped his enormous arms around all of us and just in time. It began to feel like we were starting to roll down the side of the mountain.

We were! It felt like forever that we were falling until CRRRRAAAASSSHHHH! We hit bottom. *We all bounced around inside.*

Luckily Danny's strength had protected us from really being hurt; we had gotten a few bumps and bruises, but that was all. But he wouldn't be able to protect us from what was waiting outside.

Chapter Twelve—Normal

We slowly and painfully crawled out of the log, but we wished we hadn't. We came face-to-face with two enormous Bigfoots! They were easily nine feet tall and very muscular. They were covered with thick, dark brownish-black hair from head-to-toe and had huge fang like teeth. They didn't look friendly at all. One of them was a woman.

"Danny, please tell us that they're your family and have been wondering where you've been," I whispered.

"GGGRRRUMMAAAALLLEEEE," Danny grunted as he walked over to the leader while angrily nodding yes.

I was keeping my fingers crossed that "Gggrrrummaaaallleeee" meant family in some way because Sissy, Nathan, and I were terrified. We quickly forgot about the awful fall we had just taken, when there was some rustling behind us.

At that moment another gigantic Bigfoot appeared out of the brush, from where we had obviously just been pushed. Danny went right up to him and began to grunt. It looked like he was furious with him.

The enormous Bigfoot slapped Danny across the face
sending him flying. It then went over to Danny and yanked
him up off the ground, twisting his arm behind his back. We
began to back away, but it was no use. They pushed Danny
next to us, while circling around us. They were backing us
toward another huge tree.

Within seconds there was a frightening cracking
sound as we were pushed together. On one side of us a huge
wooden plank flew up, then another, and another. Then, on
the last side, enormous metal bars clanked into place. Within
seconds a gigantic lid slid across the top of the box. We were
now trapped like animals in a cage. They had backed us into
a trap. We could see the horrible, vicious Bigfoots clasping
big, metal strips with bolts on them and then snapping a

giant lock. *It was the same kind of lock and cage from which we had freed Danny!* Danny was going crazy, howling and pounding on the heavy wooden sides.

The next thing that happened was our worst nightmare. There was a creaking sound, and before we knew it we were being hoisted into the air. Once they had us up about fifty feet, we could see them walking away. We were stuck in the worst trap imaginable with no hope of escaping!

Chapter Thirteen—Normal

"Mick, what are we going to do?" cried Sissy.

We weren't sure what they had planned, and my gut told me we didn't want to know. But if I knew one thing, it was that bad guys could always be outsmarted. We waited until we were sure they were out of sight.

"Any ideas, Nathan?" I asked.

"Just this one," he said as he dug into his backpack and pulled out the huge old skeleton key we had found when we first freed Danny.

"Fantastic! It's worth a try." I said as we carefully moved over to the lock. As we did, the entire cage tilted to one side.

"AAAGGGGGGHHHHH!" we all screamed.

"Everybody, back in the center," I yelled. "Now, we will have to move to one side at the same time Danny moves to the other to balance this thing. Ready? On the count of three, one, two, three!" We all moved as fast as we could.

Nathan and I frantically tried to get the key into the lock. We were at such an awkward angle that while I was trying to reach my hand around the bars to help Nathan I hit the edge of the skeleton key and it went falling to the ground.

"NO!" Nathan yelled.

"I'm so sorry," I apologized.

"Well, we'll have to think of something else," said Sissy calmly.

"But what?" Nathan and I asked at the same time.

"Well, what else do you have that could pick a lock?" Sissy asked.

"Just an old hairpin, but that sure won't work," I groaned.

"Give it to me," said Sissy.

I dug the hairpin out of my backpack while we sat as motionless as we could. I gave the hairpin to Sissy and she did something I never thought of doing. She pried it open and then bent it. She then carefully reached for the lock, jammed the hairpin into it, and with a few twists and turns the ancient lock popped open. Nathan and I stared at her as she smiled and nodded. I quickly unhooked the lock. We could open the door.

"But, now what?" asked Sissy.

"I don't know. We can't risk trying to get on top of this thing because it'll tip." I answered.

We slowly sat down, feeling defeated. Danny stood up and grunted; as if to say he could get us out. Within seconds he was opening the door and carefully climbing to the top of the cage. We were beginning to slide toward the open door! But just in time Danny slammed the door shut with his massive foot, and it caught. I carefully scooted over and turned the latch.

"Be careful, Danny," I yelled as he grunted. We sat in silence wondering what our fate would be. Before we could think about it for too long, the heavy wooden cage began to jerk upward.

"He did it!" Nathan yelled. Danny had managed to climb up the rope to the huge branch and was now hoisting us up. His super strength was pulling us. Before we knew it we were all the way up and he was tying the rope around a heavy branch. We carefully opened the door and one by one moved up to the top of the box. Sissy was last.

"Uh-uh. No way. I'm not climbing up there," Sissy shook as she looked up.

"Sissy, you have to. We don't have any time. Just focus, you know that you can do it," I yelled. "We have no choice…unless you want to be sold as a Bigfoot slave!"

"What?!" Sissy yelled.

"Oh, I don't know, just climb," I hollered.

Danny tapped me on the shoulder to move out of his way and reached his hand out to Sissy. She slowly held out her hand and he easily pulled her to safety. He motioned for us to wait as he put Sissy on his back and climbed down the huge tree. He climbed up and down taking us each safely to the bottom.

Within seconds of being down, I was terrified. I knew we were in trouble by the sounds that were headed our way.

Chapter Fourteen—Normal

There were large grunt sounds and then a thunderous yell came from behind us. We spun around to see that it was the bad Bigfoots.

"Run! Run!" I yelled. We took off running. We were now following Danny through the dense woods. They were right on our tail. Danny was going through twists and turns, while making sure we were right behind him.

It was hard to keep up, but what was behind us was so horrifying that we running faster than we ever had! Even more frightening was the evil Bigfoots seemed to know which direction we were going.

Before long we could see a clearing ahead. As we ran into the open space, we stopped, frozen. We were shocked. Smack dab in front of us encircling the clearing were hundreds more Bigfoots. They were in every shape and size imaginable, tall, short, young, and old…now we were surrounded.

But what terrified me more, was when I heard Nathan scream at the top of his lungs! I turned to look but he was gone. He had been caught. Now there was nowhere to turn, and all I could think of was saving Nathan.

Chapter Fifteen—Normal

Hundreds of the beasts started running straight at us! Sissy and I ducked and covered our eyes. It was terrifying! I don't remember anything, ever being so scary. It was the most horrible moment of my life. *Sissy and I were crouching together in the middle of a stampede of Bigfoot beasts.*

The pounding of the heavy feet on the ground was thunderous. It felt like the earth was moving. Dust was covering us. Suddenly I felt a huge hairy hand on my shoulder. I didn't want to look. This time we had really done it. We had wandered a bit too far and gotten too involved.

A mammoth, hairy paw was now tapping my shoulder, and the running around us had stopped. I was scared to look. I slowly peeked through my hands and saw an enormous Bigfoot woman standing next to me. Danny was standing next to her grunting and smiling. I looked at Sissy, not sure what was going on, and then saw several giant Bigfoots carefully walking Nathan toward us.

Not only had they saved Nathan, they had also managed to capture the bad Bigfoots. They had them trapped in huge nets. They were angry and grunting like wild animals. Then the largest Bigfoot of them all, he had to be at least ten feet tall, walked over to us with Nathan. The

Bigfoot was grunting at us, and it was the weirdest sound I had ever heard. Even though he was grunting—he was grunting English. We could understand him.

He told us the whole story of what was going on. We had to listen closely to understand through the grunts, but it turned out that Danny was the only living son of the two remaining Bigfoot families. Danny did have a young relative but he was an evil Uncle. This sinister Uncle, along with Danny's horrible Aunt, wanted Danny gone.

Danny was now jumping up and down with delight, clapping. Not only was his father communicating with us, Danny was thrilled his father finally knew about his vicious relatives. They had been trying to get rid of Danny for years, but nobody ever believed him.

The evil Uncle, Aunt, and another bad Bigfoot always wanted the tribe to come forward and show themselves to the world. They didn't care about the consequences. They were so determined that they would sneak away from the tribe and travel to settled areas. They were the Bigfoots that were always seen. Danny's Aunt was the famous Bigfoot woman that was caught on film. So when the greasy carnies came around to capture them, they struck a deal. They ambushed Danny and sold him for money to put the first Bigfoot out into the world. And that wasn't all; they had plans to sell off the entire tribe!

But not anymore, the evil Bigfoots would spend the rest of their lives imprisoned in exile. And, if the disgusting carnies ever came looking for Bigfoots again, they too would be taken care of.

The whole story was completely overwhelming. Here were these gigantic, apelike creatures with fangs, completely hairy from head-to-toe hovering over us. They escorted us back through the dense woods until we were almost back to camp.

We were sad to say good-bye to Danny, but somehow we knew our paths would cross again. We hugged and then they watched us move out of the forest and into the open trail.

As we waved good-bye, I was thrilled to have discovered that Bigfoot was no longer a myth. They really existed, and it was our secret, because who would believe us anyway?

THE END

Chapter One—Scary

We were in shock! This was the real deal – a genuine Bigfoot. All of a sudden the wind picked up and sand was swirling around. We were in the middle of a whirlwind.

"Ahhhggghhhh…Sand is in my eyes. I can't see!" I yelled.

"Me neither," cried Nathan.

I covered my eyes, trying to block the sand. The sky had grown dark as the clouds above us broke; torrents of rain began to fall. The beast was now angrier than ever.

"Take cover," I said, and just in time. Loud thunder boomed above us. Moments later lightning crackled and there was a blinding flash as it hit the tree that we were standing under, splitting it in two.

TTTHHHHUUUUMMMMPPPP!!!

The large branch above us fell. Nathan and I quickly moved away. The huge, heavy tree limb had landed right on top of the cage, cutting it completely in half. It was hard to see through the rain, but we could hear a tearing sound like tape. Then came the loudest growl, louder than anything I had ever heard. Suddenly an enormous fur-covered hand reached through the broken cage, and with a single motion, tossed the huge branch to the side.

Our eyes met the horrific beast's eyes. He was madder than ever, and there was only one thing to do.

"RUUUNNNN!" I screamed at the top of my lungs as I grabbed Nathan by the shirt, pulling him with me.

We began to race through the forest, trying hard not to slip on wet leaves and branches. The woods were dark and scary as thunder pounded. The beast was hot on our trail, and we could hear the roar of the semi truck. But we kept running, trying to get out of the woods.

Nathan and I tried to stay together. The sound of the truck grew louder, and the beast was still after us. We had to wipe our eyes every few minutes to see through the pouring rain. There was an open spot just ahead.

"We're almost there…we've got to hide." I panted.

"Slow down, I think we've lost him," Nathan shouted back.

My only hope was that the beast decided to go after the semi truck instead of us. Pretty soon I would find out that I was wrong – way wrong!

Chapter Two—Scary

We continued running. I looked back to see the beast but realized he must've started chasing the truck, because he was nowhere to be seen.

"We've lost him. I need to catch my breath" I gasped for air as I collapsed on the ground.

"Yeah, me too," said Nathan bending over.

"Where are we?" I asked.

"By my calculations, just through those trees … should be the carnival."

"Mick. Nathan. Over," Sissy's voice cracked through the walkie-talkie.

We practically jumped out of our skin we were so startled.

"Sissy! Sissy! Over," I said. "Come in, Sissy. Over."

"Mick, what's happening there? Over."

I told her we had found the cage with the real Bigfoot and what had happened. That she needed to stay where she was, while we tried to get back. Nathan and I began to carefully make our way through the rest of the forest toward the carnival.

We were going to have to sneak back to the Myth Mobile without getting caught by the freaks, carnies, or Bigfoot. I couldn't bear to think of what would happen if we got caught.

Chapter Three—Scary

When we finally made it to the edge of the woods, we peered out. We could see there was a gathering of freaks behind one of the tents next to the huge, grey metal trailer. They began to split up. Several of them jumped into the back of an old pickup. But instead of heading into the woods or toward the Myth Mobile, the truck went the other way. We didn't care why, we just knew we had to move and fast. When we thought the coast was clear, we began to creep out of the woods...*and it was the biggest mistake we could have ever made.*

"Over there! There they are!" I heard a man yell, as I turned to see the Snake Man pointing at us. He had come around the corner from the front of the tents. Nathan and I took off running toward the only way we could go, behind the tents.

"Under here, Nathan." I whispered, as we ducked under one of the bigger tents in the middle.

Once again we managed to shake them, but we were really taking our chances because we had no idea what we would find in the tent. It was pitch black and quiet. We were shaking as we quietly dug our flashlights out of our backpacks.

Luckily there was no one inside. The tent turned out to be storage for the carnival. We shined our flashlights around the enormous junk-filled tent. We could see old trunks, props, and even a few parts from rides. There were giant-sized, old, creepy-looking, plaster-painted parade heads sitting around. It looked as if they were cut off at the neck, and their creepy eyes were watching our every move.

It was the scariest place I've ever been in. There were old freak-show posters lining the sides. There were even old glass and metal square boxes with eerie, fake animated people in them. The whole place was bizarre. We were completely spellbound by all the old circus and carnival stuff. Until the noisy engine of the semi truck startled us. It sounded like it was outside the tent.

"Now what, Mick?" Nathan shuddered.

"The trunks…jump into one of the trunks."

We opened the huge, heavy lids on two of the ancient wooden trunks, jumped in, and quietly closed the lids. Sitting silently and waiting, I started to feel around the inside of the trunk. I didn't know what was in it, but I had the feeling that something was right next to me. I tried to figure out what it was by touching it. It had old, crunchy fur and it felt boney. I was sure it felt like something in the shape of an animal. I grasped what felt like a long, straight shaped thing, but as I was holding it...

SNAP! It broke off in my hand. The sound made me jump. I was so afraid that the noise could be heard, I sat completely still and silent, holding onto whatever it was. I was hoping Nathan was alright in his trunk and we wouldn't get caught.

Then I heard muffled voices. The freaks had entered the tent! *They were searching for us.* They would surely look in the trunks. My heart was beating so loudly, I swear they could hear it. I couldn't move. I had to sit there perfectly still...not realizing the horror that I was holding right in my very own hand.

Chapter Four—Scary

I tried to listen to what they were saying. One of the voices sounded like the Fortune-Teller, and a different voice like the Fire-Eater's, his voice was easy to recognize because it was so gravelly and raspy. But there were others. I couldn't understand what they were saying. I listened carefully as the voices grew fainter. It sounded like they were leaving. More time went by and I was right. They had left the tent, and not a minute too soon. I was getting a cramp in my leg from sitting in the trunk.

Now, I had to see what I was holding. I reached for my flashlight and clicked it on.

"AAAAAGGGGGGGHHHHH!" I screamed at the top of my lungs, and I quickly pushed the trunk open and jumped out.

"What? What is it?" Nathan screamed as his trunk flew open and he jumped out.

"A dog's leg! Look," I cried while trying to steady my hand as I pointed the flashlight into the trunk. There was the most horrible, disgusting thing. It was an ancient, mangy stuffed dog, and I'm not talking stuffed-animal dog. This grotesque thing had once been a real, live dog!

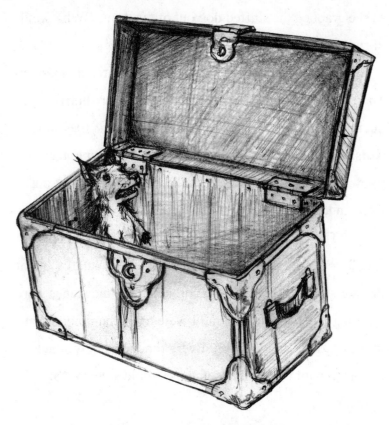

"That's hideous," exclaimed Nathan.

"Yeah, I know, and I was sitting in that trunk with it," I said, feeling sick to my stomach.

"What kind of sick, twisted person would stuff a real dog?" Nathan asked disgustedly.

"I VOULD," shrieked a weird voice from behind us.

We spun around to see the Fortune-Teller. The freaks had not left and they began to circle around us.

"My Nanooshka … my Nanooshka! They broke your leg," screamed the bizarre fortune-teller Madame Varooshka

119

as she grabbed the stuffed dog out of the trunk. "What kind of ruthless people are you?"

It was a sickening nightmare. They circled around us. Their weird costumes and heavy make-up were horrifying, but their unusual expressions and threatening smiles were worse. Before we could even think about escaping, they threw a giant net over us and yanked it. Our feet went out from under us and we fell to the ground.

They tightened the net and we felt like fish being caught. Then they began pulling us on the ground. I thought that for sure our legs would be broken. Dirt and stones were scraping our skin. Nathan and I were trying hard not to bang into each other and to sit up. Every time we did, we could feel a whip hit the net and someone would scream, "Sit down."

We didn't know where they were taking us, but wherever it was, I had the feeling we would never be found again!

Chapter Five—Scary

"Mick…Come in, Mick. Over," Sissy said repeatedly into the walkie-talkie. "That's it," she thought to herself as she grabbed her backpack and raincoat. She did a quick check to make sure there were no carnies or freaks outside the Myth Mobile, then slipped out into the rain and headed to the carnival.

Quietly and cautiously she moved through the parked cars toward the tents. She ducked down between the cars and tried to reach us one more time.

"Come in, Mick! Can you hear me? Over," she whispered harshly.

But still there was no answer; Sissy didn't know what to do now. If she got our parents involved, we could all end up being captured by these weirdo traveling carnies.

She carefully crept out from the cars and ran behind the Fun House, which still had a sign on it that read, **'DANGER—HIGH VOLTAGE—KEEP OUT— CLOSED FOR REPAIR.'**

From there she ran to the back of the nearest tent. She bent down, slowly lifted the heavy white vinyl, and peered under.

Nothing! Nothing but an empty tent and a filthy old stage. She ran to the next tent and looked under it, again nothing. She had a feeling in the pit of her stomach, worried she might never find us. Finally, at the next tent, she could hear muffled voices coming from inside. She put her ear to the tent and carefully bent down while trying to hear what was going on.

But what she heard wasn't human. It was like a small monkey or chimp sound. As she stood there trying to listen, the chimp sounds grew louder. The next thing she knew was the Bearded Lady's monkey was lifting up the heavy flap to reveal her standing there!

"Get her!!!" screamed Madame Varooshka as Sissy took off running.

But it was too late.

Chapter Six—Scary

Sissy felt a hard tug on her hair and went flying backwards. Igor picked her up and threw her over his shoulder and ran back into the tent.

"Sissy," I screamed, peering through the net.

"No!" said Nathan.

"Let go of me you freaks! Let me go!" Sissy yelled at the top of her lungs as she pounded her fists on Igor's back. It was hard to see, but I could hear her kicking and screaming with all of her might. Moments later someone was loosening the net and shoving Sissy in next to us. Then they pulled the net as tightly as they could. We were all laying side-by-side in this giant, heavy rope-bag, barely able to move let alone break free.

"Now what? What are we gonna do with these rotten kids?" asked Madame Varooshka. Her phony accent was now gone.

"I'll tell you what, we can sell them for slaves," I heard a familiar voice say. Greasy Guy had returned.

"Yeah, especially the girl, she would bring a small fortune in outer Slongovia," said Madame Varooshka.

"Outer Slongovia!?!" Nathan screamed. He had read about the horrible things that happen in that country. "Mick, we gotta get out of here."

"SHUT UP!" Greasy Guy yelled and kicked Nathan. Seconds later we heard a ferocious roar .

It was the Bigfoot! He must've been following Greasy Guy. Bigfoot stood there pounding his chest and roaring with his huge fangs glistening. His heavy fur was matted down from the rain, making him look even fiercer. The freaks froze, scared stiff, until Bigfoot began to go after them.

They quickly scattered around the tent, trying to hide in the props while screaming. Bigfoot shut them up fast. First he caught Greasy Guy and Igor and clonked their heads together knocking them out. Next it was Madame Varooshka and the Fire-Eater – he picked them up and tossed them like they were dolls across the room. After that he threw the Sword Swallower and the Tattooed Man into the trunks and slammed them shut and locked them. Bigfoot pounded his chest, grunted, then turned and stared at us.

"Mick, now what?" cried Sissy. It was hard to see, being caught like a fish in the heavy net, but I was too afraid to answer her.

Chapter Seven—Scary

It felt like we had been carried hundreds of miles, even though I knew it was a short distance outside and around a corner. Every once in awhile, the net would hit him and my face would rub against his foul-smelling, gross wet fur. It made me want to throw up. I kept hoping and wishing someone would see us. We couldn't even use our walkie-talkies to radio our parents. Our skin was raw in spots from the net rubbing against us, and we were bruised from being tangled together.

"BEEP, BEEP, BEEP!" A loud car horn went off and Bigfoot spun around. I thought maybe someone had seen us, but I was wrong. Wherever the sound was coming from, it startled Bigfoot enough to make him stop where he was, lift us up, and toss us into what looked like a big, dark hallway. We rolled onto a hard, cold metal floor and heard a huge door slam shut as the room went completely black.

"Nathan, Sissy, you guys OK?" I whispered as we tried to get untangled.

"Yeah, how about you, Mick?" Nathan replied.

"Well, now I know how fish feel," I groaned.

"No kidding! I can't move," Nathan exclaimed.

"Sissy, you OK?" I asked frantically.

"I think so ... not sure yet," Sissy said, frightened.

"Listen guys, we can't give up," I said, trying to sound encouraging. "If we could somehow move around... Nathan, maybe you could get into my backpack. I have my extra flashlight, it might still work and maybe we could find the top of this thing and get out."

Nathan and I began squirming around and we managed to move around enough for him to get into my backpack and find my extra flashlight. Sissy laid still and quiet. I was starting to get concerned about her. She seemed completely disoriented in the agonizing net.

"I think I got it!" said Nathan excitedly.

"That's cool." moaned Sissy. It was the first sign of hope that she was doing OK. What a relief that was.

Nathan flicked on the flashlight, and it looked as if we were locked inside a gigantic metal box. It had parts of old carnival rides in it. We could see what looked like chairs from the Scrambler and Zipper rides and long, broken metal poles with light bulbs stuck in them.

"It looks like we're in a semi trailer truck." Nathan said, exhausted.

"You're right. It's the trailer part of that semi cab that was parked next to the woods. Can you find the knot on this thing?" I asked.

We shifted around trying to find the opening of the huge net bag, being careful not to lose or break the flashlight. We rolled one way and then the other. We scooted around, tried sitting up, tried to kneel, but the only thing we were getting was more bruised and scratched. The heavy rope net was tight around us. We were stuck!

Chapter Eight—Scary

"Ouch! What is that huge lump that I keep rolling over?" I asked.

"Wait , that's it, Mick. It must be the knot." exclaimed Nathan.

"Ouch! Helloooo… I do believe there is another person in this fish bag," Sissy said sarcastically.

"OK, then let's all try to move around so we can get the knot on this net on top of us," I said.

"Mick, if we can just scoot, then turn about two inches, I might be able to get to it," said Nathan.

We moved around again, trying to get a good look at the tight knot. The minute we saw it we knew we were defeated. There was no way we would ever get it undone from the inside of the net. It was over for us, we were trapped.

"So you mean to tell me that you two are going to give up? Just like that? Oh well, let's not plan on dinner tonight… no, wait, maybe we should because WE ARE GOING TO BE IT!" Sissy exploded. "Uh-uh! No way. Not me, boys. I'm not being chow for any walking rug. Nathan, are you right behind me?"

"Afraid so. Glad you didn't have any chili lately."
Nathan began laughing and snorting his rare snort laugh.
With the predicament we were in, it felt good to laugh. It
was our comic relief, for a moment anyway, a very brief
moment.

Chapter Nine—Scary

TTTHHHUUUUUDDDDDDD! The entire trailer shook as if something massive had bumped into it.

"What in the heck?" Nathan exclaimed.

"What was that?" asked Sissy, alarmed.

We were completely silent for a few moments but there was no other sound. Nothing, so we went back to working on the huge knot.

THHHUUDDDD! I happened again. The truck shook for a second time and then it was still.

The thud had come from the front of the trailer, like something had backed into it. Then the entire trailer began to vibrate. Somebody had attached the cab to the trailer, and now it was driving away, with us in it!

"We're moving," I whispered.

We were beginning to bounce toward the front of the trailer.

"We're moving toward the rides and parts," said Nathan.

"Listen." I said. Sure enough, we could hear the familiar raspy voice, Greasy Guy and his evil friend were driving the truck.

It was hard to hear because we were bouncing all over the back of the truck. I was hanging onto the flashlight for dear life. We tried to listen. It sounded like they were saying something about getting out of there for good.

"What are we going to do, Mick?" whispered Sissy.

"I have an idea." I said as I managed to point the flashlight at the broken rides. "Look, can you see that sharp piece of broken metal over there on the floor? On the count of three, let's try to get over to it. Maybe we can cut the net on it." We managed to scoot over to the broken lights on a metal pole.

"OK, we haven't got much time," I said, "Sissy, sit tight and try to hold your position. Nathan, you hold that part of the net. I'll hold the flashlight and let's try to pull back and forth."

We worked quickly and the threads of the net began to unravel. The net was pulling apart! Then finally part of the net split open.

"That's it. That's all we need," said Nathan.

Once we had shredded one piece of the net, it was easy to pull apart the intertwining rope. We quickly pulled open a hole big enough for us to climb out. We were close to being free.

Chapter Ten—Scary

We managed to stand up and stumble over to the mammoth trailer doors while the truck began to pick up speed on the bumpy path.

"Where do you think they're going?" asked Nathan.

"The opposite way of where we need to be, we have to get out of here, now." I replied.

Once we reached the heavy metal doors, we grabbed the latch at the bottom of one of the doors. Together Nathan and I managed to pull it up, but the minute we did the door immediately flew open *–taking me with it!*

"MIIIIICCCCCCKKKKK!" Sissy screamed.

I held on for dear life as I dangled from the open door of the semi truck as it swung wildly back and forth. It was like a scene in a movie!

"Sissy, chill! We have to help him." yelled Nathan. "Now, run back there and get one of those broken poles with the carnival-light ropes on it. HURRY!"

Sissy bounced from side to side of the truck as she made her way to the front to find a pole.

Meanwhile, I clutched the swinging door. I was so scared I could've pooped my pants. Luckily I didn't, but every time we would hit a bump I would swing back in toward Nathan and then out again. He would try to grab me but I wasn't close enough.

Sissy ran back dragging a massive light pole. Nathan quickly tied a loop in the cord, but as he was ready to try to rope me in the truck began to slow down. Greasy Guy had seen me swinging back-and-forth in the rearview mirror. The truck came to a sudden stop and BAM! *The door swung back and I slammed into Nathan and Sissy.*

"C'mon. Let's get out of here," Nathan exclaimed as they pulled me up and we headed to the door.
Next thing we knew, we could hear their creepy voices on the other side of the doors.

"As fast as you can, on the count of three…" I said as Sissy, Nathan, and I used all of our strength to push the door open. As we did, we knocked Greasy Guy and his partner-in-crime to the ground.

"JUUMMMPPP!" I yelled, and we all leaped to the ground. There was no time to look back.

"RUUUNNNNN!" hollered Nathan.

We ran as fast as we could, dripping with mud from our jump. We had managed to escape.

Once we heard the truck engine start up again, we looked back to see it moving away. We stopped and bent over while trying to catch our breath. We were so relieved they weren't coming after us. When we finally looked up we could see the carnival tents in the distance.

We quickly moved along the perimeter of the woods, getting closer and closer to safety…*But we didn't know we were being followed.*

Chapter Eleven—Scary

"Look!" said Sissy pointing to the ground. There were massive Bigfoot prints in the mud. We looked to see where they led.

"They're gigantic. And it looks like they lead right into the woods," she said. When we looked up, we froze with fear.

"AAAAAGGGGHHHH!" Sissy screamed hysterically.

There was Bigfoot, about ten feet from us and moving right at us. Once again we took off running as he began chasing us. He was roaring and grunting so loudly we were terrified.

"There's nowhere to go," I screamed as we got closer to the carnival.

"Look, there's the Fun House! We can lose him in there." Nathan yelled. "Look for a back door."

"NOOOO!" Sissy cried. "It had a "**DANGER HIGH VOLTAGE**" sign on it."

"There's no other way. If we don't hide, we'll be caught and eaten alive. And if we run into the crowd, someone else will get hurt. Be super careful not to hit any switches," I hollered.

Once we reached the top of the steps, I grabbed the door knob, it opened!

We piled into the dark, mysterious Fun House and locked the door behind us. When I turned my flashlight on, we could see this was one scary and sinister Fun House. Not much *fun* about it...There were huge clown heads with spine-chilling faces hanging everywhere. It felt like their eyes were watching our every move. We moved up a ramp, but when we got to the top we could hear the door handle shake. It was Bigfoot! Seconds later the door was completely busted off its hinges. We could see him from the top of the ramp. He was more violent and angrier than ever, as he stood there growling.

"C'mon, we've got to hide." I whispered ... but just then ...

HAAAA HAAAA HAAAAA! HAAA HAAA HAAA! Horrible, ear deafening laughter filled the Fun House. The lights started flashing on and off, and the massive clown heads above us began moving around. Then squares of the floor that we were standing on began moving in different directions.

"He must've hit the switch." I said, trying to keep my balance.

"He did, he activated the Fun House. Don't touch the railings." insisted Nathan.

Bigfoot had heard us and now he was charging up the ramp – right for us!

Chapter Twelve—Scary

It was almost impossible to walk forward as the Fun House floor moved faster and faster. We couldn't drop to our knees or we would be pinched by the moving floor. When we managed to get to the end of the trick floor, there was a broken slide, and the only other way down was to jump down ten feet onto an air mattress below.

"JUMP!" I yelled as we all jumped at once. We landed safely and quickly rolled off the mattress onto the floor.

"Watch out," hollered Sissy as she pulled out a pin and stuck the giant air mattress. It immediately hissed as it began to deflate. Moments later Bigfoot was standing right above us ready to pounce on the mattress.

"This way!" hollered Nathan as we began to make our way through spinning barrels.

Bigfoot jumped down to the floor, breaking the old wood planks. But he immediately got up and was right behind us once again. We moved into the spinning, twirling barrels, hoping to get him trapped. But once we were in the middle of the barrels, the lights went dark and a strobe light started flashing. It made Bigfoot even crazier than ever, as he pulled on his wet fur while we began to get away. Bigfoot lifted his enormous feet and began to kick the barrels right up off the floor. Barrels were flying everywhere and the laughing sound effects continued blaring in our ears.

"Through here!" I yelled, as Sissy and Nathan moved with me.

We ran through dark swinging doors into a mirror-maze filled room.

"We have to split up and see if we can trick him," Sissy said.

We each went and stood silently in front of different mirrors in the maze. I was at the mirror where my stomach was completely stretched out. Nathan was at the super, super skinny mirror, and Sissy had an enormously long head. There were lots of other kinds of distorting mirrors around us. We tried hard not to laugh at ourselves considering the seriousness of our situation.

Once the evil beast caught up with us, we would have to stick to our quick-thinking plan of moving from mirror to mirror to completely confuse him. This was going to be our last chance.

Chapter Thirteen—Scary

Bigfoot's heavy footsteps were only a few feet away. The black swinging doors flew open, we were shaking and terrified as we gave each other a nod. Unexpectedly Bigfoot tore off one of the swinging doors and threw it across the room. His sharp fangs looked like they were ready to eat someone alive. He was roaring and growling…until he saw the mirrors. Instantly a puzzled look came over his face.

He stomped up to one mirror and made a weird, confused sound. Then he saw us! First he went straight for Nathan. All we could do was keep our fingers crossed that this plan would work.

Bigfoot thought it was Nathan as he tried to grab the mirror. His massive paws slid all over the mirror. Now he was so angry that he slammed his hand on the mirror and it shattered. His massive paw began dripping blood.

He was more furious than ever. Bigfoot began to turn in circles quickly, looking at the different mirrors. Then his eyes locked on me! I stood frozen; I thought my heart was going to pop out of my chest. Breathe Mick … just breathe, I thought to myself. Wait for the perfect moment.

There it was. Bigfoot reached at the mirror, trying to grab me around what looked like my long skinny torso and again he hit a mirror. Now he was crazed. He went completely wild. He began throwing and kicking the mirrors, knocking them all over the place! Glass was shattering everywhere as we carefully backed away, hiding along the edge of the room. Bigfoot could still see our images in the mirrors but if the beast looked toward us, we could back up into the shadows.

His fit of rage continued as he destroyed mirror after mirror. He had broken and shattered so many that we could now see a giant fuse box behind the middle circle of cracked mirrors. It had **DANGER-DO NOT TOUCH** signs all over it. The beast's fur was still soaking wet. I had a plan!

"Nathan, are you thinking what I'm thinking?" I asked.

"Yeah, if we could get him to touch the electrical box it would electrocute him," whispered Nathan.

"Exactly." I replied.

I quietly picked up a piece of broken wood and threw it over the beast's head. The wood hit the fuse box. The beast quickly turned and looked at the giant box, puzzled. Then he looked my way. We immediately ducked back into the dark. Next Sissy found a large piece of broken mirror and carefully picked it up and tossed it at the box. It hit, shattering and falling like a glistening, silver rain!

Bigfoot slowly began to move toward the box. We stood breathlessly in the shadows. He was reaching for it— his wet furry arm was just above the box going toward a piece of mirror…lower…lower…he was reaching for it… ZZZZZZZZZZZZZZZ…CHHHCHCHHCHH…ZZZZZZZ ZZZZ…FFFFZZZZZ!!!

The beast stood completely upright with his hand stuck on the box. His entire body was stiff, and then it went black, and we could see his enormous bones right through his wet fur as it stood straight on end. He had been shocked!

"C'mon, now's our chance, make sure that you don't touch a thing." I insisted.

We tried not to look at the beast; it was so horrifying and gross. We ran for the exit. We had to get out of there and fast. We found our way to the exit door and stopped to stare at the huge metal push bar. We couldn't take the chance of touching it. We could be electrocuted.

Chapter Fourteen—Scary

"What are we going to do now?" I asked frantically.

"Look, there's a chair," said Sissy. We ran over to it but it was one of the Fun House tilting chairs and it was nailed to the floor.

"What about that mask…look! Over there." screamed Nathan pointing. Over on the wall within our reach was one of the eerie, laughing, plastic clown masks.

We quickly ran over to it and with all of our might, yanked it off the wall. It was big enough that we could all hold onto it and push the door open.

"Now, whatever you do, do not let your skin or any part of you, touch the door." I stated.

We held the door open with the mask as we carefully slid out one at a time. I was last and had to be really careful not to touch the metal. Finally we were out.

We were free! It was the side door, and luckily there was nobody around. We quickly ran around to the back of the Fun House and then over to the next tent. We slowed down, peeked around the corner, and cautiously walked out front. We could see that there was a crowd gathering in front of the Fun House. The entire building was now shaking!

"It looks like it's gonna blow." yelled a carnie, "Duck!"

We could see everyone running for cover. Then there was a massive BOOM!!! Part of the roof blew off, then out of the giant hole clouds of brown and black fur erupted! The fur began floating down through the air. *The electrical box and Bigfoot had exploded!!!* Brownish-black fur was everywhere. It covered the ground and the people…and it still smelled disgusting.

"OK, let's get out of here, without being seen," I said as we slowly made our way ducking through the crowds toward the Myth Mobile. Suddenly I felt a hand grab my shoulder and it spun me around.

"Hey, kids…I've been looking all over for you!" said Dad. "Don't you have your walkie-talkies on?"

"Dad!" I said as I hugged him tightly.

"Well, I'm happy to see you, too, Mick. Look at you guys; have you been rolling in the mud? Oh well, you can clean up in the Myth Mobile because we've got to get out of here." said Dad.

"Wh…why…what's going on?" stuttered Nathan.

"It appears that the news reported a Bigfoot sighting in Bluff Creek today. So we're going to head over there to see if this myth really exists or not. Besides, there's nothing here but a carnival," Dad explained.

Nathan, Sissy, and I looked at each other, our faces grew pale. I knew we were all thinking the same thing; could there be more than one Bigfoot? But, as far as we were concerned this myth had already been solved.

A HAIR RAISING ENDING

Chapter One-Western

Nathan and I stood there in plumb shock. This oversized beast was beyond darn near anything we'd ever seen. We were scared out of our boots! Plus it stank to high heaven. Pee-yoo, the stench was bad. But this varmint was everything that folks had always talked about.

It was just layin' there. It couldn't move a muscle the way it was hog-tied. The one thing we were confused about was it didn't look like a full grown Bigfoot. Shucks, as big as this varmint was, there was something like a young'n about it. Even though its hands alone were the size of frying irons and its head was as big as tumbleweed.

"Holy smokes!" exclaimed Nathan.

"We have to set him free." I said.

"You crazy? I mean, this varmint could rip us to shreds." Nathan said as he got all upset.

"I don't know, " I answered. Just then the mighty Bigfoot shook its head no, and mumbled something from under the gag.

"Look, he's trying to speak." I said.

Just then the Bigfoot began to gesture to his mouth.

"He wants it off," I said reaching my hand into the cage as the Bigfoot leaned his big head over to the bars. "OK, this is going to smart."

"Mick, you better be root-tootin' ready to get your paw out of that cage." Nathan demanded.

I slowly reached my hand in, grabbed the gag, and yanked it off as fast as I could.

"Oooouuuuuuueeeee!" An awful scream came out of Bigfoot's jaws.

"Sorry 'bout that." I said

"Thanks, I breathe," said Bigfoot.

Nathan and I did a double take as we looked at the beast.

"Nathan, did you done hear that?" I asked.

"Yes sireee, I sure did," Nathan answered as we stared at Bigfoot in disbelief.

"You talk?" I asked.

"Roam earth two hundred years, we talk," the Bigfoot replied, "but I not two hundred years, I son, Son of Bigfoot."

"See Nathan, he's just a little whippersnapper! I knew it." I replied.

"I thank little people to untie wrists, help get out before wickeds come," Son of Bigfoot added.

"Uhhh… yeah," I replied as Nathan and I reached in and began trying to untie the knots in the ropes.

We worked as fast as lightning trying to set him free. Now Nathan and I aren't usually the gutless yellow-bellied lilly-livered type. But what happened next scared us to death.

Chapter Two-Western

Just as we were on the very last knot, Son of Bigfoot yanked his giant hands away and punched a whole right in the top of the wooden crate. Next, he stretched his gigantic hairy arm outside the crate and grabbed the heavy metal padlock and snapped it right off.

"Back up," I said quietly to Nathan, afraid of what would happen.

"No afraid," Son of Bigfoot said angrily.

"No. You kiddin'? We're not afraid," I said, trembling.

"I captured no more by bad man. Now, must go home." said Son of Bigfoot.

"Where? Where's your homestead?" I asked.

"Not sure. Disobey father. Father say Bigfoots can never leave secret land or stolen by hairless peoples. I disobey. Wanted to see ghost town. Then wickeds come, take Son of Bigfoot away for a traveling show."

"Ghost town? Where's a ghost town?" Nathan asked.

"Middle here and Bluff Creek," Son of Bigfoot answered.

"That's just a stone's throw from here," I exclaimed. "We can help you find your way back."

"Ohhhh…I plum don't know about this, Mick."

"Why on earth not?" I asked.

"Just how do you suggest we get there?" asked Nathan.

At that very moment we heard the sound of a horse moseying our way. We ducked behind the cage and peeked out to see Cowgirl Sissy arriving.

"Howdy Sissy," I yelled, jumpin' fer joy.

"What in tarnation are you two doing? And what is that ferocious monster doing with you?" Sissy asked.

"You are mistaken. He ain't no monster, he's Son of Bigfoot. But listen, we've got to get a move on, time's a wasting," I replied.

Nathan and I jumped on Sissy's horse and Son of Bigfoot followed us back through the thick forest toward the traveling road show. We realized Son of Bigfoot and Sissy were going to have to wait in the woods. Nathan and I dismounted and snaked our way toward the back of the tents, not knowing we were being staked out.

We saw three horses and ducked down behind the trough while untying them. We were lucky that they were already saddled up.

"Hey, what d' ya think yer doin?!" someone hollered.

As we turned to look, I could feel my heart in my throat when I saw that it wasn't anyone we would want to be messin' with!

Chapter Three-Western

"Nathan, jump on!" I screamed and we jumped on the horses. "Giddyup!" Grabbing the reins of the third horse, we took off. We were already at a full gallop and I could feel rocks whizzing by my ear. I could see Greasy Guy and his rustlers with slingshots aiming right for us, but it would take a lot for those outlaws to catch up to us.

We got to the edge of the woods and Son of Bigfoot jumped on. We took off faster than a speeding train following the trail. I could tell by the sun that we were heading in the right direction.

The landscape quickly changed to desert. Sand and rock formations surrounded us as we rode past prickly cactus, lizards and snakes. There were vultures circling over head, hoping that we would be their next meal. I could see we were nearing Devil's Pass and knew we had to keep moving because this would be the perfect place for a hold-up.

"Mick what's yer horse's name?" asked Sissy.

"Don't know. Reckon he doesn't have one." I replied.

"You mean to tell me yer goin' through the desert on a horse with no name?" asked Nathan.

"Reckon so, Nathan, reckon so."

We were coming to a curve with a fork in the road. Son of Bigfoot was now leading the way and insisted we take the path less traveled.

Sure enough, as we passed over the ridge and though the copper-colored canyon, what looked like a mirage was actually Dead Man's Gulch.

"Look. Up yonder," I hollered as we slowed down to a canter.

"I can see it," yelled Sissy.

"Me too," bellowed Nathan

There it was, the most frightening ghost town known to man. Son of Bigfoot began hootin' and a hollerin' with joy. As we got closer, we slowed down, we knew we were right. Cuz we started passin' old, crumbling covered wagons stuck half in the sand with broken wheels and shredded covers. There were old barrels, coffins, animal bones, and cattle skulls. I was hoping they was cattle skulls. There were lots of them.

For some reason, this town had really suffered some bad ordeals, but what we didn't know what was in store for us.

Chapter Four-Western

At that precise moment, Sissy's horse started rearin' up and Sissy was a screamin'.

"Hang on, Sissy!" Nathan yelled.

"Settle down, boy! Settle down. Surround her." I shouted.

"We can't," hollered Nathan. "There's a rattler!"

Sure 'nough, crawling out of one of the old cattle skulls came a huge rattler.

It was coiled and ready to strike while Sissy kept holding onto the wild horse for dear life.

I was scared for my kin. It was my responsibility to watch this filly, but this snake was mean and mad. Its long slithery body was as tight as could be, and its razor sharp fangs glistened in the beating sun, ready to sink those teeth into anything that moved.

While we were getting near Sissy and facing the rattler, Son of Bigfoot had rode behind it. He slowly and carefully dismounted his horse and within seconds grabbed the hideous snake by its rattler, swung it over his head, and launched it hundreds of feet away.

"Whew! That was a close call. Thanks." I said to Son of Bigfoot.

"I thought I was a goner," said Sissy trying to calm her nerves.

Once again we started to mosey down the path toward what was once known as the most ferocious town in the West, Dead Man's Gulch. It was the perfect name for it. It had once been a peaceful town until it became a settlement for the most ruthless, evil lawmen that roamed the earth.

It was said that in its last days there was nothing but gun fights, hangings, and hold-ups and the town was left for dead. It remained a ghost town ever since. When passers by tried to explore it, they had been driven away by vicious spirits chasing and terrorizing them. I was hoping that wouldn't be our fate. Reckon I wasn't hoping hard enough.

Chapter Five-Western

The minute we got into town, we went to the well and pumped it to get some water for the horses.

"Don't believe that old thing will still be working," said Nathan.

But sure enough, it did. Fresh, clean water started spilling out, which was kinda strange for such an old well in an abandoned ghost town.

"I feel like we're being followed," Sissy said suspiciously.

"Me too." said Son of Bigfoot.

Nathan and I felt the strange feeling too as we looked around the abandoned town. There was an old saloon, a general store, a boarding house, blacksmith, livery, post office, theatre, sheriff's office and jail, a hotel, a bank, and three funeral homes. That immediately clued us in to what must've been the town's most prosperous business – dead people.

"Well, Son of Bigfoot, I guess this is where we have our farewell," I said.

"Heck, Mick, we still have an hour or so before we head back…

What do you say we wander a bit before we go?" asked Nathan.

"Alright by me," exclaimed Sissy.

"Sounds good, how about you?" I asked Son of Bigfoot.

"That why I come here in first place," Son of Bigfoot replied.

We tied up our horses and headed into the saloon. The steps creaked as we walked in, and the old saloon doors that hung crookedly with peeling paint squeaked loudly.

Inside it was easy to imagine this place in its glory days; it must have been one booming saloon. I could imagine it filled to the brim with cowboys.

A beat up, old piano stood in the corner, although it was missing a few keys. There were some broken tables and chairs and old glasses. Playing cards scattered the floor. The long, wood carved bar still stood with old bottles and a faded, scratched mirror. But the middle part of the bar was missing, as if someone had taken the whole thing out. The wind was rustling through the broken windows and the shredded curtains were flapping.

"What'll ya have, Cowboy?" asked Sissy, joking as she picked up a broken, half tray from one of the tables.

"I got a hankerin' for a sarsaparilla, lil' missy," I smirked.

"Hey there little lady, I could use something to wet my whistle, too," added Nathan.

We were all laughing and joking as we pretended that we were living in Dead Man's Gulch...

CRAAASSSHHH! From somewhere upstairs something fell. We all froze.

"What was that?" whispered Sissy.

"Probably a raccoon or some kind of animal," answered Nathan.

It was an animal alright, but the kind you would never, ever want to mess with!

Chapter Six-Western

We continued joking around in the deserted saloon, forgetting about the mysterious noise. But the next sound we couldn't ignore when we heard the stairs creaking.

We quickly spun around. Standing on the stairs were half-rotted, dead-looking cowboy corpses! But they were alive! The Undead! And they were making their way down the stairs right straight at us.

"RUN!" I screamed at the top of my lungs, and we all took off for the swinging doors and got stuck. We couldn't all fit through them at the same time.

"Spread out!" I said as we struggled and shimmied through them. Once outside in the bright sun on dusty Main Street, we could see there were two more creepy zombie-like cowboys coming in either direction.

There was nowhere to go except straight ahead. We ran across the street right into Miss Mabel's Boarding House. When we got in, we bolted the door shut, and Son of Bigfoot moved chairs and tables over to block the door. We ducked down and peered out the window. I was keeping a look-out and I could see that they were headed right our way!

Their clothes were tattered and rotted, and it looked like you could see the bones on their faces. They moved slowly, draggin' their feet. They were surrounding the boarding house!

"Mick, any ideas?" asked Sissy.

"Not at the moment. I knew there were ghost towns but this is crazy. Got anything, Son of Bigfoot?" I asked. As I turned to lean back, my hand hit an old spittoon that went rolling across the floor. As it rolled, a thick, brown, gooey liquid poured out of it.

"Fresh spit," said Nathan. "Somebody has been here recently."

"That's a fact!" I said as we heard the creepy dead cowboys climbing up the porch of the boarding house. "Head for upstairs!" I yelled.

"You go! I hold back." said Son of Bigfoot.

"No." I declared as I pulled him and he followed along. We ran up the rickety old stairs. Once we got to the top, we realized we were trapped. We ran from room to room tryin' to find an old fire escape. When we found it, we saw it was broken off. We slammed one of the boarding-room doors, looking around feverishly for an escape. There was no way out.

Chapter Seven-Western

"We're trapped." I exclaimed.

"What about the roof? We could climb up and go to the next building, they're connected." insisted Nathan.

"I stand corrected. Great work, Nathan. C'mon, we gotta move fast." I said as I leaned against the door. We could now hear the zombie cowboys coming up the stairs. The whole thing was strange and horrifying, and before long we could hear their pace had quickened.

Bigfoot moved out first, being extra cautious so's not to fall through the decaying wood.

"I'm afraid," hollered Sissy.

"Quit yer bellyachin', Sissy! If you don't git then the jig is up," I said as the footsteps drew closer.

When Sissy heard them, she crawled out the window toward Bigfoot and up onto the roof. Then Nathan and I went last. We could hear the door starting to break apart. Just as I was about to head out they had broken through! One of them grabbed my boot but I kicked back and hit him in the face with my spur. Then I quickly got a move on. Once on the roof we carefully ran, dodging holes and rotting wood!

"Head toward the barn!" I yelled.

As we neared the barn, we could see that it wasn't attached to the roof of the building, but it looked like we could jump.

The horrible undead were now climbing out onto the roof.

"OK, I think if we get a running start and jump across that gap then we will surely make it!" I said.

"I not so sure," said Son of Bigfoot.

"We got no choice, those bad eggs are hot on our trail." insisted Nathan.

"Well, I ain't dyin' with my boots on so let's go." hollered Sissy.

We backed up and began to run as fast as we could. Our huge leaps carried us across the gap, and one by one we landed safely on the barn roof. But within seconds there was a loud cracking sound.

"Heck! It's gonna break through." I yelled as we started to stand up, but it was too late. Within seconds the entire roof gave way and we all began to fall.

Chapter Eight-Western

We plummeted into the barn. Falling, falling, and then BOOOOMMMMPPP! BAM! CRUNCH! CRACKLE! We landed on a massive mound of prickly, old hay.

"Ouch! That smarts." whined Sissy.

"Thank goodness this hay was here…Never mind y'all, no time for a chat. Cowboy up! Let's go." I screamed.

We brushed off our spurs and quickly scrambled down the barn ladder to the bottom level. Once down, Son of Bigfoot threw the ladder out of the barn. We had seconds to git somewhere and hide, but we didn't know where. Then we saw the Prosperity Hotel just across the way.

We ran across the street and ducked inside. The splendor of the hotel was all but gone. There was shredded, peeling wallpaper, old velvet couches with springs and stuffing poking out, broken lamps, and faded, torn rugs scattered about. The one thing that was intact was the huge chandelier that hung above us in all its faded brass glory. We quickly made our plan.

Nathan and I lassoed the big chandelier, and then we gently pulled it back toward the top of the staircase. Son of Bigfoot grabbed on and held it from a corner. Then Sissy went into the old kitchen and found an ancient canister of molasses. I began pulling rusty nails from the walls where broken pictures had been hung, and picked up shards of glass from the broken windows. Sissy then quickly covered the floor with the smelly, old sticky molasses, and I scattered all of the old nails and glass on the molasses. Next we moved the old couches against the wall while Nathan kept a look out for the undead.

"Here they come, and they look as mad as hornets!" hollered Nathan. I could see the creepy undead makin' their way up to the hotel door. We were ready for them. They slowly opened the door, and walked into the hotel.

"Yoo hoo…here we are, boys…and we're fixin' to git you!" Sissy yelled from the top of the stairs.

Nathan and I were crouched behind the couch we had placed behind the molasses and nails. It was an outlandish scheme, but if it worked we could capture the undead and escape.

As they entered the hotel, we peeked from behind the couch and could see them up close. Heck, somethin' wasn't right. Little did we know that in seconds we would find out just how wrong things in this ghost town really were.

As they started to head toward the stairs, Son of Bigfoot let out a tribal scream and swung on the chandelier right into them, knocking them to the ground smack dab into the molasses, nails and glass. We jumped from behind the couch while they were busy trying to get off the nails, glass and glue-like molasses and ran around them with a giant rope, tying them up.

"We did it, partners!" I shouted. "We caught the ghouls of Dead Man's Gulch!"

"We sure did," smiled Nathan.

"And how!" said Son of Bigfoot.

"Well boys, I don't know if it's exactly the ghouls we captured," said Sissy as she pointed to the gang we had just tied up.

"Ya know, Sissy, something tells me yer right," I answered as I walked over and yanked one of the hideous. masks off of a fake ghoul.

Sure enough, it was Greasy Guy.

"I had a hunch it was them." I said. And at that instant we froze as the hotel door flew open.

Chapter Nine-Western

In walked the Sheriff from a nearby town and his Deputy.

"Jeez, are we ever glad to see you." I said.

"That's no balderdash." said Nathan.

"I think it's the other way around." said the Sheriff. "We can't thank you enough for catching these ruthless outlaws. They've been terrorizing this old ghost town for years. Now the jig is up. We've been tryin' to make Dead Man's Gulch a historical landmark but every time we do these desperadoes scare all the tourists away."

Nathan pulled their masks off. Looking at the pile of badness sprawled across the floor; we could see that along with Greasy Guy, was his evil partner and some of the other carnies and freaks. They were all in cahoots.

"They even stole them there horses from a dude ranch in Bodie. Fact is they stole the whole darn carnival." said the Deputy.

"That ain't true. We's innocent," yelled Greasy Guy.

"Don't you run yer mouth anymore" said the Sheriff as they began to pull the outlaws to their feet.

In all the commotion, I had forgotten about Son of Bigfoot, and him bein' around real folk. I looked around alarmed. Sissy caught my eye and motioned to the window. I walked over with Sissy and Nathan, and out yonder I could see a cloud of dust and a horse galloping off into the sunset with one lone hairy rider.

"He said to give you this," said Sissy as she handed me Son of Bigfoot's hat.

"Yes siree, Mick, he wanted to thank you. He knows his way home from here and said he will always be a partner and ride with you." said Nathan.

With that we thanked the sheriff, mounted the horses, and headed out into the sunset. It was time for us to git a move on, far away from Dead Man's Gulch.

Happy Trails!

Chapter One—Talk Show

"… ladies and gentlemen Helen Generous!!!"

"Thank you! Thank you very much. Wow. OK, have we got a show for you today." said Helen. "I can't even believe it! We are actually going to have an entire family of Bigfoots right here. Yep, the real myth, uh-huh, Bigfoots … or is it Bigfeet? Huh? What is it? Does anybody know? Bigfoots, Bigfeet. I'm not quite sure. I'll have to look into that, but isn't that amazing?

What's that? Wait one sec, I can't hear the lady in the front row. She has a question…How do I know they're the real thing? I don't know, how do I? I guess I could pull on their fur or something, ya know, make sure it's not a mask. Heck, I'm pretty sure they're the real thing. Cuz we also have the family that discovered them, or I should say the boy, Mick Morris, with his best friend Nathan and cousin Sissy. They'll be joining us. You know there've been claims for hundreds of years, all kinds of people saying they spotted them. Well, now we find out, I shouldn't say we, we didn't find out anything. It's the people from the 'Myth Solver Show' who actually found out. Oh, I hear the music, let's dance!"

Chapter Two—Talk Show

"Woo hoo that was fun! Did you like those new moves? OK, you know every day we chat, but not today. Let's bring out our special guests, shall we? Here they are the cast of the 'Myth Solver Show,' the Morris Family!"

"Hello, hello. How's everybody? OK. Wow! Quite a group here, I think we are going to need more chairs. Have a seat everyone." said Helen, "Hi, Mick."

"Hi, Helen!"

"Mick, everybody, Mick Morris. And aren't you the one who actually discovered the Son of Bigfoot?"

"That's me. But I had help, my best friend Nathan, and my cousin Sissy helped me discover him," Mick added.

"Uh-huh. And when you say discover, you mean like, you actually found him, is that correct?" Helen questioned.

"That's right. See, Nathan and I had Sissy staked out in the Myth Mobile…" continued Mick.

"OK, I just gotta tell everyone, the Myth Mobile is an RV they travel around in while uncovering myths and legends. Here's a picture of the Myth Mobile."

"It's big. I guess to fit everyone, right? It's cool. So go ahead, how did you come across the Bigfoots, or is it feets?" asked Helen.

"I guess Bigfoot is correct. You see Sissy was in the Myth Mobile while Nathan and I were out looking for the evil carnies…"explained Mick.

"Uh-huh, aren't they the guys who actually kidnapped Son of Bigfoot?" asked Helen.

"Yeah, really bad guys. Now they're in jail."

"Yeah, so you not only managed to solve the myth of Bigfoot but you, Nathan, and Sissy actually put away a major crime ring? Isn't that right? Asked Helen.

"Yeah, I guess we did," Mick answered.

"So how do you guys feel about all of this?" Helen asked Nathan and Sissy.

"Well, I just can't believe I'm here Helen. I'm a huge fan, and I'm just busting at the seams," gushed Sissy.

"Well, don't do that, that would messy." said Helen.

"How about you, Nathan? I mean, what do you guys think about discovering the myth?"

"Well, it's truly amazing that we found him."

"Yep, unbelievably amazing, and you are all amazing. Hey, you guys out there are lucky, too, cuz you are seeing it here live. The first time ever a real Bigfoot family! When we come back …" said Helen.

Chapter Three—Talk Show

"OK, we're back and I'm a bit nervous! I am, this is the moment … we are happy to introduce to you the actual, living myth…the Bigfoot family!" announced Helen.

The audience stands applauding while an entire family of five Bigfoots walk out onto the stage. They bow and clap, wave at the audience, and sit down. Son of Bigfoot sits next to Mick.

"Wow … woweee! Amazing. This is history. Isn't it?" Helen announces from the stage. "Oh my gosh, I don't know what to say. Well, I guess I should say sorry those seats are a little bit small. Well, probably smaller than what you're used to anyway. So how are you?"

"We're good. Good, Yep, Fine…" the Bigfoot family replies.

"Son of Bigfoot, well, first off, what is your real name?" Helen asks.

"My actual name is Bert Bloffo, and this is my mother Betsy, my father Bernie, my twin sister Bertha, and my older brother Dawg."

"Dawg?" asks Helen, "Why Dawg? I mean not even Bawg? You know so he fits in the rhyming thing?"

"Yeah, ha-ha-ha, that's his nickname because he always comes home from picnics with hot dogs, his real name is Bob." replied Bert.

"OK, well I gotta ask, like how did Mick convince you to come out in public?" questioned Helen.

"Mick actually met with producers and studio people to make sure that if we went public we could do our own story," Bert replied.

"Uh huh. Really? Wow! So you are producing your own film? And how do you two, Uhhh…Mr. and Mrs. Bigfoot, Bigfeet, feel about that?" asks Helen.

"We're pretty excited about it. We just bought a home in LA, the script has been approved," answered Mr. Bigfoot.

"Yes, we just bought Jennifer and Brad's old place," replied Mrs. Bigfoot.

"I did hear that. That's great. Hey, I know a really great interior decorator. In fact I even bought you a little housewarming gift." said Helen.

"You did?" asked Mrs. Bigfoot.

"Uh-huh. I got you this welcome mat especially made for your new home. It says, Wipe Your Big Feet Here. I hope you like it." said Helen.

The audience breaks out in laughter.

"I love it! Thank you," said Mrs. Bigfoot.

"Great…and we'll be right back."

"Wow, what a treat! Thanks for joining us, Bigfoot—uhhh, feet family. We can't thank you enough Mick Morris and the 'Myth Solver Show.' Good luck on the rest of your myth-solving missions. That's our show for today! Be sure to join us tomorrow when we have ..."

Stay Tuned

181

182

183

189

191

The terror that the dark woods bring...sightings of
massive, frightening beasts known as

BIGFOOT

Bigfoot Facts

Bigfoot names: Yeti, Sasquatch, Skunk apes, Maricoxi, Almas, Yerin, Hibagon, Yowie, Wendigo.

Some reported sightings since the 18th century have occurred in: United States, New Zealand, Venezuela, Hawaii, Africa, Russia, China, Tibet, Japan.

Size: 7-10 Feet

Weight: 500-1,000 pounds

Foot size: Up to 27 inches.

Actual population: Unknown

Habitat: Remote wilderness areas across the world.

Special features: Ape and humanlike features with thick brownish black hair from head to toe, with extremely long arms and huge feet.

Bigfoot is said that it could be a pre-historic survivor of the Gigantopithecus, which was a relation to man from over 300,000 years ago. Others, from different parts of the world are said to resemble Neanderthal man and hominids.

People continue to hunt for Bigfoot in search of hard evidence.

LEARN TO DRAW BIGFOOT

FIELD NOTES:

A giant teddy bear – he's not! Bigfoot is an enormous beast who has been seen by people for hundreds of years. There is even a famous video of Bigfoot walking through the woods. In the video, as well as by those that claim they've seen him (or her) it's reported that he's a combination of human and ape; with long, thick reddish brown, or dark brown hair from head to toe, and extremely long arms with huge feet – hence the nickname "Bigfoot." He is said to be 7-10 feet tall, and weighing anywhere from 500-1000 pounds. He's supposed to be smelly, too! That's why one of his nicknames is Skunk Ape, along with some other names: Yeti, Sasquatch, Yowie and Wendigo.

It's reported that this huge, ape-like creature could be a pre-historic survivor of the Gigantopithecus, which was a relation to humans over 300,000 years ago. Yikes! That's a long time to be in hiding – especially when you are so big. Lots of people say that they've discovered Bigfoot's gigantic foot prints; some have even made plaster molds of them. So, we know this beast would have a super hard time buying shoes; since the imprints that have been copied are an average of 2-3 feet in size. And, can you imagine how smelly these big feet must be? Yuck!

STICK
FIGURE

SHAPES

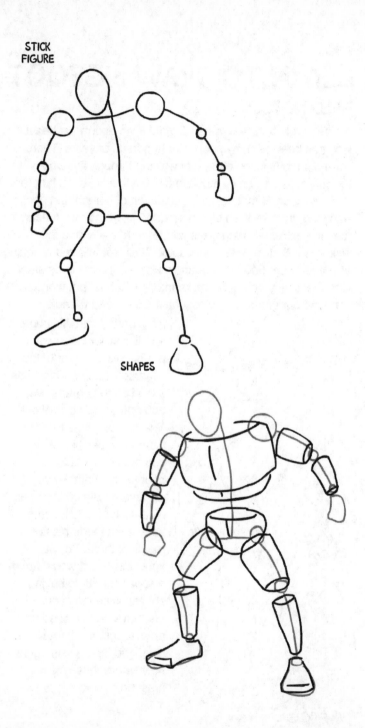

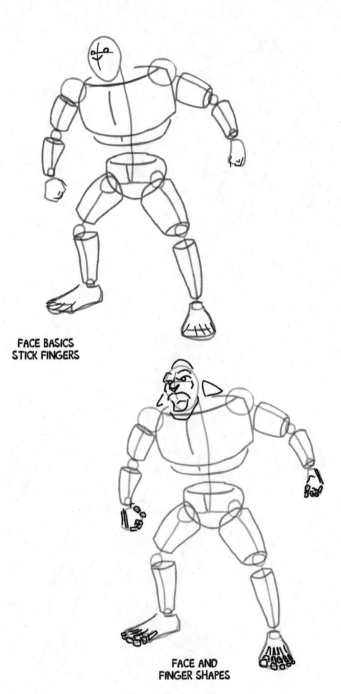

FACE BASICS
STICK FINGERS

FACE AND
FINGER SHAPES

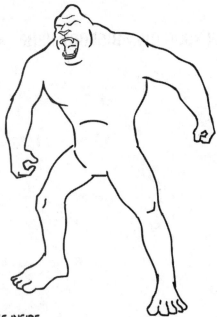

ERASE INSIDE
GUIDE LINES

EXCEPT FOR THOSE YOU'LL
NEED FOR DETAILS

DETAIL

STEP-BY-STEP ART
INSTRUCTION FROM OUR
"HOW TO" SKETCHBOOK,
'SKETCH THE MYTHS.'
80 PAGES OF FUN!

DRAW YOUR OWN BIGFOOT HERE

SPOTLIGHT ON STYLE...

We love *The Muppets*!
Jim Henson was an inspiration in so many
ways. We came up with our Muppets
inspired Bigfoot by adding bits and pieces
from some truly memorable characters
like Cookie Monster, Animal, Fozzy Bear,
and a little of Sweetums. Henson's work,
and his characters are timeless - he was
an artistic genius.

Would you like the Breges to visit your school? They have an awesome presentation that will keep you laughing while you learn about art, writing, and reading!

Have your teacher or school administrator email staff@teambcreative.com for more information on their fantastic presentation!

"Westwood students had the privilege of being visited by authors this spring. Karen and Darrin Brege held two assemblies during Reading Week. The Breges promised and delivered high-energy, interactive performances which included drawing, reading, and writing mixed with humor and comedy. We couldn't have asked for better assemblies."

Published by the
Lansing State Journal (www.lsj.com)

About the Breges

Karen Bell-Brege and Darrin Brege - author,
illustrator, married, parents, crazy, fun
comedians. Together they write, draw, and
inspire children to read and follow their
dreams. They are passionate about the
importance of laughter and the arts.

Karen also teaches improvisation, and Darrin
creates art and illustrations for top global
brands, along with posters and books.
Every year they present at hundreds of schools,
events, and associations. They love scary stories
- so here's one for you!